Born and raised in East London, trained in Martial Arts, professional patisserie and Law, DI Whittle began her writing through the love of Hans Christian Anderson tales from a very young age.

Blessed with an autistic son, writing and reality became inter-meshed and new worlds began evolving through life experiences and shared dreams inspiring books, pictures and poetry.

This book is dedicated to the fondest memories of my nan, Sylvia Whittle, a nurturing, kind, profound reader and matriarch. With a special thanks to my son, Rio, for being a beacon of light and showing me the true sense of being different.

DI Whittle

X RAY VISION

AUSTIN MACAULEY PUBLISHERS™
LONDON • CAMBRIDGE • NEW YORK • SHARJAH

Copyright © DI Whittle 2023

The right of DI Whittle to be identified as author of this work has been asserted by the author in accordance with sections 77 and 78 of the Copyright, Designs and Patents Act 1988.

All rights reserved. No part of this publication may be reproduced, stored in a retrieval system, or transmitted in any form or by any means, electronic, mechanical, photocopying, recording, or otherwise, without the prior permission of the publishers.

Any person who commits any unauthorised act in relation to this publication may be liable to criminal prosecution and civil claims for damages.

This is a work of fiction. Names, characters, businesses, places, events, locales, and incidents are either the products of the author's imagination or used in a fictitious manner. Any resemblance to actual persons, living or dead, or actual events is purely coincidental.

A CIP catalogue record for this title is available from the British Library.

ISBN.9781398442009 (Paperback)
ISBN.9781398442016 (ePub e-book)

www.austinmacauley.com

First Published 2023
Austin Macauley Publishers Ltd®
1 Canada Square
Canary Wharf
London
E14 5AA

Thank you to my son, Rio, for helping me understand.

Finally, to Austin Macauley for making the publication possible.

Table of Contents

Chapter One: I Am Ray	11
Chapter Two: Ready, Steady, Books	17
Chapter Three: The Stop Button	23
Chapter Four: Fortnite Royale	28
Chapter Five: Black and Blue	37
Chapter Six: Driving Me Crazy!	39
Chapter Seven: Twins	42
Chapter Eight: Chalk and Carrots	48
Chapter Nine: Cat and Mouse	55
Chapter Ten: St Thomas's	58
Chapter Eleven: Last Orders	63
Chapter Twelve: Late Night Trolling	68
Chapter Thirteen: The Thames	70
Chapter Fourteen: Wiggly Wiggly	75
Chapter Fifteen: The Fish Counter	79
Chapter Sixteen: Missing	82

Chapter Seventeen: Oh for Fish Sake!	87
Chapter Eighteen: Silver Linings	91
Chapter Nineteen: The Nativity	93
Chapter Twenty: Hollow Words	100
Chapter Twenty-One: Indecent Exposure	104
Chapter Twenty-Two: Up and Away	109

Chapter One
I Am Ray

Ray had an affinity for art and not much else…

He was on the autism spectrum; it made him think outside the parameters of 'The Social Norm'; at times, he acted a bit odd. He often upset people that did not understand his condition, and he had a natural ability to ask myth-defying questions that no one could answer.

"Mum…Where do eggs come from?"

"Chickens!"

"I see. Mum…Where do chickens comes from then?"

"Eggs!"

And so, it would continue…but that didn't bother him.

Ray had Tourette's syndrome; he gurgled and grunted, usually at the same time sporadically throughout the day; his throat often ached from the harsh irritation of repetitiveness. His 4 ft 4 inches slender body had involuntary jerking actions, and unbeknownst to him, he blinked 100 times per minute, but that didn't bother him.

Ray lived a normal life just like any nine-year-old boy, with his hardworking mum Veronica; she always tried her best for her only child, and today was no exception. For his tenth birthday, Ray only wanted some friends over to play, but Veronica wasn't going to let going into double digits slip by without celebrations. A science celebration. She had decorated the house, invited a few school friends over and turned the kitchen into a makeshift laboratory. Each little professor had their own white lab coats and goggles, £4.99 a set from amazon was a bargain! Throughout the airy, amply sized kitchen/diner, she hung colourful streamers and hazard tape; she draped cooked spaghetti and shrivelled mushrooms, mimicking worms and mulch over the island counter. She overfilled chronicle flasks full of bubbly red and black-dyed lemonade; she generously stuffed party bags with goodies, used jelly frog moulds and made Lindt chocolate eyeballs for dessert. She stayed up late wrapping a black bag full to the brim with pass the parcels.

A rented smoke machine fogged the front door for their guided grand entrance. Ray was excited; he was aware time was ticking on, and nobody had yet arrived yet. But that didn't bother him.

The lemonade bubbles began to pop, and the chocolate eyeballs began to take on a less solid shape in the afternoon heat and the smoke had dwindled to a mere faint mist. They both remained hopeful as Veronica waited for a call, or message back from the parents she had tried to reach. This didn't bother Ray.

Time ticked by silently, and the house was eerily quiet, the only noise was the clanking of the Victorian-style radiators. There were no calls or messages.

Two hours later, they safely assumed that nobody was coming. Ray sat with his goggles on at the table alone. Veronica brought a smartie covered cake over to Ray with a lit candle. Ray blew out the candle making a wish before running upstairs. That bothered him.

Ray slammed his bedroom door shaking the mid-terraced townhouse. His sad confusion etched deeply on his face, along with the indentation of the goggles. He dove underneath his fort that he had made from blankets, sheets and an old curtain pole.

"Nobody likes me," Ray sobbed to himself; he began hitting his head out of frustration – one hand after the other; he blamed his head for nobody showing up. Abruptly stopping in his tracks, Ray spied Jeff the dragon eyeing him up. Jeff was a plastic toy that realistically resembled an authentic Hungarian Horntail from one of his favourite movies; a movie that he had watched more times than Veronica cared to remember.

"You like me, don't you, Jeff?" he asked. In Ray's imagination, Jeff had a muddled Scottish accent, one that he vividly recalled from a movie Veronica watched more times than Ray cared to remember, there was some strange men with skirts and face paint that roared like dragons. When Jeff would talk, he would roll his R's and this amused him to no end.

Ray dug his nose out as he laid on his belly whilst he freely swung his legs, as they played. Veronica always told him there was not any gold up there so he shouldn't be digging so hard! Ray seldomly listened; he enjoyed it and continued to scavenge around his nostrils each in turn After Jeff suggested that they get into Ray's rocket shaped bed, to do some galaxy exploration, he agreed. Wiping his hands along the once immaculate now peeled wallpaper, Ray slipped into bed with his trusted friend.

They visited the outskirts of Jupiter flying at breakneck speeds cutting through the drifting meteors that dotted the atmosphere. They endured a rough landing on a bumpy crater on the surface of the moon, before enjoying a toasted marshmallow from the sizzling heat of the sun. When they came back down to earth, it was dark outside, and the stars shone the brightest Ray had ever noticed. He jumped on his bed with Jeff, both rolling back into the mattress as they landed their spaceship safely. Veronica popped her head in to check on Ray; he was gone in play world; unnoticed, she slipped back out.

Ray lay staring at the constellation scene decorated on the ceiling. Veronica had painstakingly replicated a picture that Ray drew of the night sky. He had said that Veronica's mum, who he never got to meet, lived in a star that watched over him at night. Ray was comforted by this. Night after night, he went to sleep with grandma twinkling above.

He lay looking up at Grandma on the ceiling. His vision was interrupted by a streak of light catapulting past his bedroom window. Jumping out of bed, he thudded on the floorboards; he stamped heavily over to the window gazing at the sky.

"It's a shooting star!" he gasped.

"Jeff! Jeff!" He brought Jeff over to the remenance of the star's burnt outline. Ray's jaw ticked violently downward with innocent excitement.

"Oh, you missed it!" Ray paused for a moment before getting back into bed with Jeff. Ray lay staring at the window. Almost as a light bulb would switch on, a star pinged high in the sky outside. It pulsated in time with the beat of Ray's heart. He jumped up again, bringing Jeff with him this time.

"Look!" He exclaimed. The light was so bright that it stood out from the dim twinkly blanket that lined the night sky. Ray felt the unity of him and the star; he believed it was looking directly at him. He patted his chest in time with the light. The light began to hasten as did his heartbeat. The once bearable light was now so bright, he was squinting to keep it in view. Ray contemplated calling his mum but was stuck to the spot, mesmerised by the anomaly. The light gave one last beam of light, before it exploded with smaller rays of light blinding him temporarily; they quickly dispersed as Ray fell to the floor. He scrambled back up to look, but the light was gone. Jeff, who was balancing on the windowsill, saw everything. Ray picked him up, shook him roughly and asked him what had happened. Jeff refused to talk, obviously in shock Ray thought. They both stared out the window for what seemed like forever, before Veronica came in with a pair of light pyjamas and a toothbrush already pea'd with toothpaste.

"But I brushed my teeth yesterday." He sighed. After a quick bath, Veronica hugged Ray tightly and gave Jeff the mandatory kiss on the nose before she tucked them tightly in bed. Veronica whispered in Ray's ear:

"Happy Birthday, my love." She could not look at him as the tears welled in the corner of her eyes.

She left quickly leaving the door open a crack. Ray thoughtlessly lay in bed, mind fixated on Grandma above before he rubbed his eyes and fell asleep.

Veronica wiped off her poorly applied make up; she was not a girly girl in the slightest, but she thought she'd make an effort for the day. "What a waste!" She scowled. She loosened her hair doughnut, gliding out the pins releasing a curly mass of well-maintained auburn hair. She cursed as she slumped back on the headboard.

Heartbroken for Ray, Veronica cried into her pillow that night.

Chapter Two
Ready, Steady, Books

It was Monday morning, the first lesson of the week.

Ray refused to ask for help. He sat on his hands, tightly tucked under his bottom supressing his tics, trying his best not to draw attention to his Tourette's. The other children knew exactly what they were doing; they sat with straight backs, concentrated learning faces plastered on, workbooks on the table, with their pencils freshly sharpened. Ray didn't want to look silly in front of everyone by asking Mrs Mayover to repeat the class instructions, so like always, went with the flow, looked awkwardly busy whilst he copied off clever clogs Catherine, who sat within eyeshot.

The sound of the pencils scratching the paper, the crisp turning of the pages were getting louder than a bellowing trumpet in Ray's head; he clamped his teeth and tightly sealed his lips; he could no longer hear his own thoughts. Today, Ray was feeling particularly sensitive. His eyes were sore, and the vibrations were almost deafening. He covered his ears self-soothing himself to a much happier place, a gentle tap on the shoulder awoke him from his daze.

It was Lolly, the teaching assistant, assigned for Ray's one-to-one support. Lolly always rescued him just at the right time; she was his safe person. Lolly looked at him with her familiar kind face, effortless beauty and wavy blonde hair.

"Shall we take some Ray time?" she asked softly. Ray nodded in relief before scrambling out the classroom, Lolly in tow.

Outside in the humid air, Lolly watched over Ray wiping away the globules of sweat streaming down the back of his neck. He scuffed his shoes as he dragged his feet on the asphalted, marked playground. Lolly never asked too many questions or frustrated him; she let him speak and didn't finish his sentences, which was one of his biggest bugbears. Lolly always spoke to him clearly with no recanting of big words; she instead spoke and explained them thoroughly. Whilst he was with her he never felt 'Special' or 'Different' as he had often overheard usually in whispers from the grown-ups. With Ray's extraordinarily sensitive hearing, not too much went amiss.

"Do you need a few more minutes before we go back?" Lolly asked.

"3.8 minutes," Ray replied counting from thumb to pinkie, ensuring it was long enough for everyone to finish timetables before he returned.

"Okay, 3.8 it is!" Lolly agreed.

Ray practised his hopscotch falling short of the last square, tucking and rolling towards Lolly; she came to his aid offering him a helping hand. Lolly's dainty hand always smelt of bubble-gum hand sanitiser; he took a sneaky sniff. Lolly laughed, before she said, "We have art after literacy this afternoon." Ray's face filled with excitement.

Ray was at his happiest when he was painting, drawing and creating. Dubbed a Junior Picasso, the entire class and teachers alike would always marvel at his talent; the effortless brush strokes on canvas, the 4D dimensions from pencil to the paper was faultless. Lots of his drawings and creations lined the school corridors.

"I got way too much outside germs on my hands!" he exclaimed.

Looking thoughtfully, he peered at his hands before wiping them roughly on his white shirt.

"Much better." He smiled.

They slowly walked across the empty playground, passing the climbing apparatus. Ray stared at Lolly's shirt.

"Did you eat magical fruit?" he said curiously, brain cogs carefully ticking over as he thought of what to say next.

"Magical fruit? Like from Jack and the Bean Stalk?" she asked, confused Lolly pouted her bottom lip as she shook head.

"Yeah, for breakfast?" Perplexed, she brushed off the playground debris from Ray's shorts. Lorraine Cuttle had known Ray since the day he was born; being his mum's best friend helped their rapport at school, he felt entirely comfortable with her. This bond also meant she knew Ray well; he could have a very vivid imagination and from time to time be fond of tall tales. Tall tales were lies. Lolly had strategically moved away from the harsh taboo word that Veronica disallowed in the house, as Ray had associated it as being a bad word. Bad words stressed him out, so there was a pool of replacement words they used instead. 'Tall tales, silly goose, Ray had his elephant feet on, teddy-tired eyes, or simply, Ray time (for quiet time)'. They were soft, yet to the point. Lolly stretched her loose-fitting satin shirt painted with brightly coloured jellybeans; she looked at the pattern and instantly related the two.

"Guess I did." She giggled.

Lolly slipped Ray back into the classroom before heading off for a quick bathroom break.

Mrs Mayover knelt on her good knee next to Hasnat. As the new student, he had only been at Redwood Academy for a week or two; he had already been moved from his first class as he was having troubling settling and refused to go back. The move into yellow class would be a better fit, the head teacher thought, and today was his first day.

Hasnat would get the familiar funny looks he was now accustomed to wherever he was, along with the sniggers that made him conscious, just conscious, he was long past getting sad. However, the boys in the other class had been smart and relentless, kicking him under the table when the teacher wasn't looking, and troubling threats of playground beatings were all too much. Hasnat had a chronic skin condition. Fish Scale disease, in itself not a complete rarity but to the scale Hasnat suffered was in the medical world a rare occurrence. The delicate flakes of skin would shed continuously as it grew seven times the normal rate of the average person. The skin wept and bled when he bent at the joints, which caused him agonising pain; he needed to be pumiced and moisturised at least five times a day. Icepacks were always at hand for particularly excruciating days, and his deep wounds were often bandaged and dressed to prevent infection. Hasnat was notably physically different, his mind functioned within an average range, yet children tended to stay away through fear of contagion or lurgies as they would tease. Hasnat was still avoided like a plague, but somehow, this he had gotten used to. The most popular girl in the class, Ariel, had thought that perhaps he was actually a merman that needed to be in the water, whilst Elliot, the infamous class bottom scratcher, believed he was from another planet waiting to go home (he actually thought it was pretty cool!).

Ray was on Hasnat's table desperately trying to get his attention, phlegmy coughs and falling off the chair, being as disruptive as possible wasn't working. Hasnat pretended to pay no attention.

"Boys and girls, literacy hour!" Mrs Mayover chortled with her exceptionally large underbite; the class echoed with groans with one quiet 'yesss', hissed in the background.

"Two people sharing! Table one, you first," Mrs Mayover said. The children scrapped their chairs on the non-slip lino, marvelling at the shiny hardback books, table five shot them sideways glance of jealousy. Table one was always first they grumbled.

Cautiously, Hasnat approached Ray who was frantically trying to not make eye contact.

"Hi, hi there, you want to be my partner?" Hasnat asked, his voice higher pitched than normal. Ray nodded he was more than happy with someone actually volunteering partnership as opposed to the obligatory pairing. Ray blushed with delight unable to keep his eyes from darting all over Hasnat's skin that was on the cusp of flaking off.

Sitting together at the table, they were instructed to take turns reading a paragraph each with their partners. The chatter of the children echoed through the filled room. Lolly returned looking slightly paler than before; she had a smile full of happiness as she watched Ray and Hasnat nattering away.

"So, do you think that frogs are like baby chickens with no fur, because of allergies?" Ray asked. Hasnat was excited by this.

"Of course! Like alligators are baby dinosaurs that didn't grow, because they have ozone allergies," Hasnat responded. Both boys were in awe of each other's genius; they scribbled down their findings in their workbooks. Their once stranger ship was now turning into a budding friendship.

Chapter Three
The Stop Button

The Stop Button was roughly a thirty-minute walk from Ray's school.

Every day after dropping Ray off at Redwood Academy, Veronica Vision would park her car opposite the school. She'd take a vigorous stroll through the high street of traders setting up for a day's work. Stopping off only at a local patisserie, she would grab her morning soya latte, and, on a Friday, she would treat herself and the workforce to freshly baked pastries.

Veronica had worked at The Stop Button since Ray was a few months old; it was convenient as it worked around school hours. Ray had long been a welcomed guest when work was conducted out of available child care hours; he worked as chief button counter for the team dividing out the orders, and he was allowed to roam freely in the Stop Button's yard that had a small fish pond with koi carp. The small shop was on a quaint street adorned with marigolds and lush plants cascading from wooden window boxes, set amongst other small family-run businesses. Veronica had become a skilful worker crafting handmade buttons, of pure gold, silver, platinum, pearl and the odd time in larger batches – quality plastic. Veronica designed unique buttons for A–Z listed celebrities, from actors to their stunt doubles, to royal sultans and sultanas, to esteemed businessmen and women from every corner of the world. Anyone who was anyone got their buttons from The Stop Button.

Veronica, Karen and Wendy worked long days all week to fill the orders, so much so, they often worked weekends in the shop. It wasn't uncommon to take their projects home to complete the overflow from the busy week. Veronica would work late nights when Ray was fast asleep for extra money; she would finish each button with finesse fit for a professional button designer, no matter how tired she was. She did this not only for her love of buttons but moreover, to make sure the mortgage was paid on time and there was good food on the dinner table. There was always a chance for the odd family treat when there were extra jobs on and perhaps a trip to Clacton-on-Sea for the weekend if they lived frugally enough.

However, over the last few weeks, Veronica's absence was becoming a problem! Ray's behaviour was erratic and the endless appointments with medical professionals was staggering. Yearly dentist check-ups, fortnightly trips to psychiatrists and six monthly trips to the optometrists all due at the same time made it difficult for Veronica to meet the Stop Button's demands. Veronica's mind wandered constantly, whilst her work performance was mediocre at best. To top it all off, the boss's son kept making niggling comments every time he shuffled past; this was starting to become bothersome.

"Gettin' paid for not workin' might as well go down the job centre!" he'd sniped.

"Taking advantage again I see!" he would say loudly, directing the comments at everyone and no one in particular, when the girls would take a break.

"Can't wait till I take over. Big changes a comin!" He'd smirk.

Mrs Taste on the other hand was a firm, fair, native German woman. Ruler straight silver hair fell just short of her ears, her dark pinprick eyes magnified by the bifocals that she wore attached to a daisy chain that clung to her neck. Mrs Taste was shaped like a ripe avocado, and she refused to wear any clothes that had been made in the last three decades. The business had been purchased over 42 years ago, initially as a tailoring shop which gradually dwindled as Taste's signature, bespoke buttons gained popularity. At 72 years old, she was considering her early retirement.

Mrs Taste had two grown-up sons, Maxwell 'The Great Loaf' as she would affectionately snide, a replica of his father, god rest his soul and her eldest, Herman. Herman was her pride and joy, a successful IT consultant, married with four children; he lived with his family in a budding Mountain Town in a Swiss village, visiting the UK infrequently. Maxwell on the other hand at 29, lived off his mother's modest fortune. Unlike his mother, he wasn't fair nor was he interested in buttons; he was interested in paper, printed paper with numbers on it. The 'Butt Shop', as he privately called it, would need a complete overhaul. He envisioned the shop having its own social media account on every platform, and it shouldn't be a Button Shop. No, No, it should be a virtual arcade where he and his friends could stay n' play all day, with aliens and nonstop accolades. It was going to happen no matter what; he'd egg himself on, and he was just the man to make that happen; he only needed to bide his time; he could virtually taste it; it was that close.

Mrs Taste, unlike her eldest, was not fond of her youngest son; he only skulked out of the house when his weekly allowance had run out. Maxwell never lifted a finger unless it was to button mash, and if she refused to give him any money, he would hang around the shop until he became such an annoyance to her and insulting to the staff that she would eventually give in.

Veronica just made it through the door as the grandfather clock chimed 9 am.

"By the skin of your teeth there Fraulein!" Mrs Taste laughed hoarsely, in her fresh as the day she came to England accent. In a flurry, Veronica set down her handbag, pulled her magnifying glass down, supped at the lukewarm tea Wendy made her and got straight to work.

A minuscule shaped peach, oval dots, two engraved flicks and the cherry on the button was complete; it was placed onto the small conveyor belt that rotated the length of the shop; it trundled off, before coming back moments later empty; it journeyed to Wendy to paint precise speckles of colour before it went through the drying machine, only 704 left to go…

Veronica took pride in her work; it was the one thing she had been really good at. Being crafty, creative and quirky, she tried hairdressing before falling short at the vertical roll; she turned her hand to floristry, however, plants seemed to wilt at her presence, even events planning never went according to plan. Nothing stuck, the only thing that fit like a latex glove was crafting buttons, and she loved the hard work that came with it. This was in stark contrast to Ray's dad. When Veronica had met Kevin, he was a fleeting actor, a job a month if he was lucky. He was destined for stardom or so he liked to say; his ultimate claim to fame was once appearing in a reality TV show, before being asked to leave in the first week of the show for being a bore and sleeping all day. He had dreams of Hollywood; he was hellbent on getting to America to appear in a medical drama (he wasn't even sure which one) before making his big debut in a Hollywood blockbuster. The dream would come true and Veronica would be eating mincemeat whilst he ate steak he'd often argue. By all accounts, she had heard through the grapevine that he had made it to America. He joined a talent agency, with an opportunity to carry out some on-going extra work; he didn't hesitate leaving when Ray was six months old. His phone number no longer worked, and he never responded to countless e-mails Veronica had sent; she only knew he was alive and well through his parents, who sent a Christmas card once a year, notably always cashless. The day he left, he not only took Ray's opportunity at having a father to play with in the park, the bedtime stories, the showing how to stand up to have a wee, he also took her jewellery whilst she slept her expensive family heirloom and cleared out Ray's piggy bank.

Mrs Taste carefully packaged the completed button orders. Meticulously, she gave them a final sleeve buff and a spit shine; she did a thorough quality inspection with an eyeglass, before bubble wrapping each. Finally, it was packaged in a padded envelope with a pricey invoice attached; it was now ready for courier collection.

Veronica sat in the cramped staffroom at lunch finishing her sandwich; she was reading the local newspaper when she heard an almighty crash on the shop floor.

Chapter Four
Fortnite Royale

It was Sunday morning and Veronica was taking Ray for a treat day. He was one hour into his Fortnite Battle on the XBox 360 when he had won a new skin and had reached level 237. A new achievement. Ray was in the firm belief that if he competed, he could win a competition, no doubt, his mum would be so happy with the prize fund at stake. Highly overstimulated, Ray's Tourette's syndrome had gone into overdrive ticking with excitement; he could barely hold the controller still through the shocking vibrations.

Peeping through the crack of his bedroom door, Veronica braced herself, five more minutes and she would have the gruelling task of asking her son to turn off the XBox! Ray was only allowed two hours a week on the XBox, any deviation was a momentous uproar. Expecting a tantrum or a screaming fit, she was locked and loaded, prepared with the theatre tickets for *Fortnite the Musical.* A bit of culture mixed with modernity Veronica thought could bring them both together in a shared interest.

"Come on, Raymond, finish that game; we're going!" She bit her lip as she braced herself.

"NOOOO!" he yelled, stamping his feet.

"I need 11 more minutes; I could win a million pounds and then you could buy nice shiny handbags." Veronica smiled; she needed a new handbag; her tattered shoulder bag had seen better days, but she had made do with the same one for the past three years. She snapped out of her real leather-covered daydream.

"No elephant feet please! I have a surprise for you," Veronica said enticingly, waving the tickets although no one could see.

"Surprise? What surprise?" he asked curiously, keeping one eye on the TV.

As Ray was thinking about his surprise, a sniper hiding in a nearby tree executed his dancing banana character with one shot. The banana was no longer dancing, and Ray was no longer smiling. He whipped his neck around and let out a screech in Veronica's direction.

"Aaagggghhh! Look what you made me do!" He lobbed his remote controller through the air in defeat; it veered towards the TV, walloping the corner of the screen. The colours of the TV leaked through a hairline crack spreading like a rainbow; he held his breath, wincing, waiting for a reaction.

"Now that's enough!" Veronica frowned deeply as she raised her voice bursting open his bedroom door; Ray was scared he didn't plan on breaking the TV; he knew this meant no Fortnite. No Fortnite made him more disappointed than the actual breakage. He had the look of fear in his face, which softened Veronica's tone.

"We will deal with the TV later. Get your shoes and socks on," Veronica said; she sighed at the sight of the TV as she handed Ray the tickets to the musical. Ray was far more compliant, still on edge from his little outburst; he hugged tightly the tickets to his chest as he smiled forgetting all about the TV. Looking in his room, it was going to cost a small fortune to fix and a large percentage of their monthly budget.

Ray was having trouble with his shoes; Veronica loosened the backs, slipped her finger in whilst Ray slid his foot in and tied his laces; she looked into his round face, ruffled his floppy sun-kissed hair and gave him a squeeze; her boy was her world.

"We'll go out for dinner after. Anywhere you wanna go?"

After slipping out in the interval, Ray apologised over and over.

"I'm sorry, Mummy–Mummy, I'm sorry. Sorry!" Ray exclaimed trying not to look at his mum's red face.

"Hey, don't be a silly goose! You don't need to apologise. I should have realised it would have been too loud. 'I'm sorry'!" Veronica apologised as Ray slipped his hand deep into her jacket pocket; he held her hand tightly keeping both of their hands warm.

"No – it was just. Strange. I dunno." Ray struggled to find the words; they were in there, just jumbled in a mixed salad, and he was trying to pick out the cucumber seeds with chopsticks as he often imagined it. He tried to explain it to Veronica, as she tried equally to understand. Both no wiser to each other's ramblings.

"People were hiding in the walls. Stuff was moving and it was…" he continued. Veronica patted him comfortingly on the back, letting him know that it was all right, and he needn't say another word; she understood so far as she was going to right then and there.

As a single working parent, Veronica found it difficult to strike the right balance, being a mother and managing a full-time job wasn't easy, notwithstanding understanding the complexity of a child with autism. Everything took longer. Days had to be consistently structured and deviations resulted in revolts. She questioned herself, if the strategies that she used were helping? Was Ray actually making progress? Was the school doing their best for her only child, and what she should do for the best for his uncertain future? It riddled her with guilt that she should be doing more. There was no book, blog, article or journal written for a boy with autism, learning difficulties and Tourette's syndrome who loved Fortnite, anything to do with mythology and had a dragon called Jeff.

Today was a learning curve as was everyday with Ray. Crowds, loud noises, too many people and confined spaces were an accumulative NO GO! Singular maybe, all together an explosive combination! And that was precisely what had happened. Ray let out bloody screams; he wailed and flailed, drawing attention from across the theatre from a sea of worried, mostly annoyed faces and distracted actors that stared as he shouted strange, obscene things across the room.

"Dusty old bones!" he yelled.

"Dead people in the floor!" he shouted across the theatre, as the children and their parents looked chilled to their cores scanning the floor for the people.

"Look, look! People behind the curtains!" he shouted pointing towards the stage. It was a real showstopper. The crowd applauded when they made their hasty exit.

It was dusk when Veronica and Ray walked down the near empty high street towards a row of lit shops; people were gathering outside restaurants and pubs for their evening meals.

"Where would you like to eat?" Veronica said as if nothing had happened. She had not uttered a murmur since they left the theatre; she was stuck in her own thoughts. Ray shrugged nonchalantly; he knew where he wanted to eat but was acting coy.

"How about La Roca, pizza for you, pasta for me? Extra cheese and pineapple!" She laughed as she tickled his armpit; he slowly warmed to her affection.

They sat in the only empty table in the packed Pizzeria; it was rustically decorated with natural beams and soft warm lighting; it had a wood burning pizza oven in the middle of the restaurant that was the focal point of the room. The tables were nicely laid, with red and green napkins being placed neatly in their laps on arrival.

Ray made a swirly pattern in his foamy hot chocolate; dipping in one marshmallow at a time, he seemed overly pleased with the destruction of the swirls. The big cup and the floating confectionary were enough to keep him happy until they ordered their food, or so Veronica thought as she sipped on her glass of wine, that was going down quicker than she anticipated. Whilst they waited Veronica spoke plainly with Ray hoping the distraction of something sweet would help him talk freely.

"What upset you in the theatre?" she asked her eyes full of concern. Ray shrugged; he finished dipping his marshmallow before he began colouring the napkin with crayons. The muscles in his face twitched nervously; he knew Veronica was watching him. His Tourette's normally flared up in times he felt under pressure.

"The bones were laying in the floor, piles and piles – you know them dry bones! There were people everywhere hiding and like changing clothes, why? I could see – I could see boobies and booties," he whispered in embarrassment.

"It was weird! It wasn't nice, and I didn't like it, and I needed Ray time!" Ray finished the sentence without taking a breath. Veronica held his hand tightly.

"I'm so sorry. Maybe it was too much for you; next time, I will think a bit smaller, maybe a mid-week movie? It'll be quieter, and we can get some popcorn?" Veronica said as she felt a wash with guilt, hoping she hadn't scarred him for life. Another tick off the never-ending failure list, a self-pitying thought she tried to brush off.

Veronica was lost; all the support groups she had been to had not prepared her for this; the useless books she had read, the parents that she conversed with, all pointless! No two children were the same, and Ray was exceptional; she had known that since the day he was born. She felt like a skimming stone on a still lake, going somewhere but ultimately going nowhere and then sinking after skipping courageously. Veronica thrust a menu at Ray distracting herself from her unhelpful thoughts.

"What ya eatin?" Veronica asked as if she didn't know.

"Pineapple pizza! With extra, extra, extra cheese!" Ray panted with excitement. Beckoning a waiter over Veronica began to order; Ray eyed him from head to toe from his messy, mousy brown hair to his scuffled plimsoles as he jotted on the notepad.

"One medium pineapple pizza and lots and lots of cheese for Raymond here! I will have a spaghetti carbonara. That's it, thank you," Veronica said handing back the menu.

Ray interjected, "And garlic, cheesy bread please!" He grinned an even cheesier grin.

"Anything else?" the waiter asked.

"Are you a superhero?" Ray interjected.

The waiter confused for a moment, replied confidently, "Maybe! Are you?" he questioned raising a curious eyebrow.

"Me? No! You must be! Metal knees, metal head! That's a superhero, or supervillain!" he said looking rather worried at the later. Veronica mouthed a silent sorry towards the waiter.

"Don't be. He's spot on! I have two bionic metal knees and one legitimate helmet head! I had an awfully bad accident see, trying to save a cat out the tree, broke a lot a bones! So, the doc put a plate in my head and two brand new knees, and Ta Daa, here I am! The Warrior Waiter!" he said knocking his head. Ray's mouth dropped wide open.

"How did you know that, Ray?" Veronica asked. Before Ray could answer, the waiter pointed to the other end of the restaurant to a barely visible newspaper print mounted on the wall.

"After my surgery, I was back to work in two weeks, that's why they call me the Warrior Waiter! Free BIG scoop of ice cream for people with good eyesight today; you've earned it!" He shook his head laughing as he went to put their orders in the kitchen.

"Wow! I can't believe you saw that from all the way over here! I'm impressed! Don't need your eyes tested! Gonna cancel that appointment!" Veronica joked, patting Ray in congratulations. Ray stayed silent; he looked around constantly, unconsciously fidgeting and colouring until his food arrived. The waiter set the plate in front of him, which he stared at with immediate disgust!

"I don't want that one!" he said pushing the plate away none too gently. The waiter stepped back as the scene unfolded.

"What's wrong? It's your favourite pineapple and cheese," Veronica urged pushing the plate back.

"Nothing!" he said crossing his arms looking away defiantly. The waiter cast a judging eye over Ray's bad behaviour. Nasty little so and so, he thought to himself.

"Well, eat it then, Ray!" Veronica said sternly; her patience was thinning as she spoke through her gritted teeth, fully aware there were watchful eyes. A plate tussle began between mother and son before it tipped over the edge with a restaurant-silencing smash, splashing the young couple opposite with globules of tomato sauce and splattering over the waiter's already dirty plimsoles. The couple gave them a menacing glance whilst dabbing with a napkin before returning to their meal. The waiter apologised profusely to the other table, immediately leaving to fetch a dustpan and brush.

"What's wrong with you?" Veronica angrily whispered across the table, behind her hand.

"WHAT'S WRONG WITH YOU? HE DROPPED MY PIZZA. IT HAS GERMS AND NOT THE GOOD ONES!" Ray yelled as he stood up; Veronica gently pressed his shoulders down, bottom connecting back on the chair.

"You just dropped your pizza! Nobody else dropped your pizza; I just watched it come out the kitchen." Veronica frowned.

"I SAW HIM!" Ray insisted loudly.

"Tall tales! You stop this now for the love of!" Veronica pleaded recoiling into her white smart tomato sauce-covered blazer; she had had enough for one evening, but it was too late.

"IT IS N.O.T! – I DID, I DID! WHY DON'T YOU BELIEVE ME?" he yelled as he stomped on the pizza in frustration almost sliding in the mess. Trying desperately to calm him, embarrassed and concerned they were again the highlight of the evening; she turned a bright shade of pink.

"Can I just get the bill?" she asked the waiter as Ray continued his mulching.

"No charge," the waiter said hurryingly.

"Are you sure?" she asked credit card in hand ready for a quick contactless exit.

"Just leave, your son is upsetting the other diners. Needs some stern discipline, that'll sort 'em out!" he said with a look of abject horror at Ray's behaviour. Veronica's face changed quicker than the wind; she put a worrisome, protective arm around Ray who was now consciously focused on the people staring at him. How dare he. She looked squarely at the waiter with wild eyes, before she one-handed tossed over the table towards him.

"Now we're both upsetting the diners," she said aggressively before they made their getaway. The entire restaurant watching as they breezed through.

"What about my ice cream?" Ray chimed as Veronica quickly led him away.

Chapter Five
Black and Blue

Mrs Taste nursed her sore backside with an ice pack. Her hip and leg were different graduating shades of green, purple and yellow. Fortunately, there were no broken bones, just a sprained wrist and ankle and a bruised ego. Slipping on a button, who'd have thought it?

Propped up in her bed, she moaned as she awkwardly swallowed her potato soup. Mrs Taste's friends had rallied around, even the girls at work had made sure they visited and did their bit. She had her meals premade for her, her sheets were washed and pillows fluffed. Maxwell, her youngest son, was nowhere in sight; normally, you could never get him to leave the house, yet since she had been confined to the house, he was like a hotel guest, in late at night, out during the day.

Mrs Taste swigged on a glass of water as she swallowed down her medication; she quickly fell fast asleep. A while later, a loud creak alerted her that someone was in the room. Peeking through the slits of her eyes, she could see Maxwell skulking around her room in the shadows.

Thinking she was asleep, Max poked around in her belongings, first ruffling around in her house coat pocket. Nothing. He then rummaged in her handbag on the dresser.

"Looking for something?" Mrs Taste said startling Max. He laughed nervously falling into the dresser.

"Oh, Mum, I thought you was asleep. Scared me! I just wanted to borrow your phone; I need to make a quick call. Mine's dead" Max explained. Mrs Taste pointed to her phone beside her on the nightstand.

"Ah, ah, thanks, I'll bring it right back." Max took the phone sheepishly and left the room.

Mrs Taste felt useless; she had never been in bed so long and had to be reliant on other people. Eager to get back to work, she wanted to cry; she snivelled as she fought back the tears. No time for crying. Stiff upper lip, she repeated to herself. Her frustration was reaching boiling point; she was a simmering pot, and if Maxwell was up to what she'd thought he was, it was about to boil over.

Chapter Six
Driving Me Crazy!

In Veronica's mint condition SUV, Ray was buckled in the back seat. Veronica took great pride in keeping her car clean and pristine; her late mother had once told her that 'If you take care of things, things will take care of you', a saying that she regimentally lived by, her vintage clothes were testament to that. Arms folded, Ray stared out the window in silence, eyes flashing at every moving silhouette outside.

Ever since his birthday last month, Ray's mood swings had intensified; his behaviour ever more erratic and precariously unpredictable. Veronica could only assume that he had been hurt by nobody turning up to his party, and this had a profound impact on Ray. It felt like she was tiptoeing around on eggshells, avoiding arguments at all costs; they felt like they were always just a wrong word away. The last thing she wanted to do was upset Ray, but today she had to ask; she clicked down the radio.

"Ray," Veronica began. He stayed silent.

"Ray," she said a little louder, biting her lip in frustration before turning to him, momentarily taking her eyes off the road. Ray was staring unblinkingly out the window; he started to take shallow breaths that rattled deep in his chest. Unable to speak, he was intently focused ahead on the corner house, only able to see the shadow of the movement behind the ill-fitting curtains. Ray squeezed his eyes tightly as his body seized with fear; he let out a scream as he deeply scratched at his own face. Veronica's foot was heavily teetering on the accelerator before she suddenly slammed on the brakes at the sound of his sudden scream. The car behind slammed into her, another car hit that car, and then a car behind that nudged them all forward into the traffic light pole followed by loud headlight crunches from the impact.

In a blind panic, she screamed at Ray.

"ARE YOU OKAY?" her eyes checking him over; Ray pointed over at a house across the street with a distinct quivering of the lip; he let out a shudder.

"Thaaat la-lady ne-ne-eds help for her, for her h-er blood!" he said stuttering every word.

Veronica looked to where he was still pointing; there was just the usual curtain twitching, spying the accident.

"What the hell are you talking about, Ray? There is nobody over there. I haven't got time for this. Just be quiet while I go sort out this mess!" Veronica held her neck in discomfort as she quickly exited the car. Ray sat still as a statue, not taking his eyes off the corner house, the lights flicked off, ending a harrowing ordeal inside. His tense shoulders were hurting his body; he held his stomach in sympathy pain, as he tucked his head firmly between his legs; he silently cried, his trousers wet.

The aftermath saw disgruntled drivers swapping insurance details, taking pictures and noting names. Veronica got back in the car slamming the door; without saying a word, she slowly drove back home with the bumper in the boot.

Alone in his room, Ray blotted out the world; it was his room and he had put up the do not disturb sign on his door handle. Dragon wallpaper hung sparingly as space plants swung from the ceiling amongst the painted stars, the bookshelves adorned a selection of magical tales and fables, whilst a cosy corner had a shabby fort and, his now broken TV, and games were stacked neatly in a built-in cupboard.

Ray read and re-read the Dragon Wagon, his favourite book, a dragon that drove a dilapidated hotdog wagon, having endless mishaps and adventures. This was Ray's world – faultless and adult-less; nothing was beyond his control and here he felt safe. Ray was playing jovially with his roaring dragons that flapped weightlessly underwater guarding the new city. The dragons and mermen had just collaboratively built Atlantis from Lego with some tap water from the bathroom. Suddenly, they all met a very sticky end, pulverised by a mer-eating giant teddy squid, whilst the treacherous dragons fled to safety. He laughed at the destruction. Ray was the curator, and tonight, he was not creating a happy ending.

Immersed in mythological creatures, Ray never felt alone in his room full of wonderment; the events of the night were all but forgotten as he fell asleep on the floor.

Chapter Seven
Twins

After an evening of silence, Ray and Veronica went to bed, neither would get a full night's sleep. Veronica tossed and turned. She cried. She sniffled. She hugged her childhood soft toy Scruggs, a tatty rabbit, finding small comforts with every squeeze of her old friend. Her mind raced as she thought of Ray's screams, what was going on in his little mind? How was she going to get the bumper back on? She visualised the list of expenses that needed paying for; it was mounting up to a big chunk of her budget. Telly, now car, anything else she pondered.

Ray woke up in his bed in his pyjamas little after 2 am; he was sure he fell asleep on the floor; he lay staring at Grandma star on the ceiling. He watched as the planets hypnotically swayed from the draft, before falling back to sleep.

One warm toasted strawberry pop tart coddled in a napkin, a prepacked backpack and a shoulder bag full of essentials, Ray and Veronica were ready for a new day. The morning carried on like yesterday never happened.

Looking at the rear of the car, Veronica sighed quietly to herself. It looked ugly. An overwhelming sense of self-pity washed over her; every time she had something remotely nice, it got ruined, and to top it all off, she now had a bumper in her boot. Her car was officially bumper-less and her ego was officially bruised.

Buckling up, the pair took their normal route to Redwood Academy; the building traffic was making them late; it was unusually heavy for this time. Veronica impatiently tapped her steering wheel trying to peer ahead to see what the holdup was; the cars moved at a turtle's pace. The emerging TV reporters lit up in their eyes; they were set up on the side of the road in their drones. There were lights, cameras, and indeed, there was action. As they approached the exact scene of their car accident last night, it had become clear that more than one incident had occurred at the very same spot.

Police tape cornered off one side of the street, keeping the prying eyes at a distance, as the reporters filmed from across the street. A white forensic tent morbidly sprung up outside the entrance to the corner house. A bright yellow incident sign was resting on the pavement giving little to no information. Ray watched in terror as uniformed officers questioned neighbours on their doorstops and stopped passers-by. He felt immediately as if he had done something wrong; he slid just below the window line out of sight to avoid detection. The passing car drivers and their passengers rubbernecked at the mysterious going-on. Veronica glanced a harrowing stare at the unfolding scene before covering her mouth.

"Ray, did you see something here last night?" she whispered loudly. Ray still hiding, answered only.

"I want to go to school."

Veronica gripped the steering wheel without another word. Her mind raced with curiosity. Did Ray see something in the house? She didn't even remember driving the rest of the journey to school.

Arriving at school dead on time, Ray spied Hasnat through the railings hurtling towards him, waving manically. Veronica waved Ray on a cautious wave as she made her way into the school office; she didn't fancy a social worker on the doorstep after the school sees the scratches on Ray's face. She also needed to speak to Lolly. This midweek dinner invite to all her family and friends in the group WhatsApp was out of the blue, and she wanted to know what Lolly was up to.

Veronica briskly walked the well-maintained shrubbed pathway to the school office. A young pretty face strained a smile in front of her blocking her path, stopping her in her hurried stride.

"Oh, hi, Veronica, I haven't seen you in ages! How's Ray doing?" the school mum asked. Veronica bypassed her face, her down gaze revealing the woman's skimpy outfit.

"Oh, hi! Ray's fine, after you didn't bother to come to his party, return my phone call, or answer my text, or, or come to think of it, even respond to the note the school put in your son's book bag; he's just super, thank you so much for your concern!" Veronica said at lightning speed; she smiled falsely before detouring around her, leaving a huffing, embarrassingly startled parent.

The school receptionist, Mrs Wiggle, a plump middle-aged, well-dressed woman, sat slumped behind the glass at reception not acknowledging Veronica. She tapped gently on the glass to which Mrs Wiggle held up a wrinkled index finger.

"I'll give you one minute, you old prune," Veronica muttered under her breath. Lolly appeared before Mrs Wiggle had even looked up, letting Veronica through the security doors.

Veronica sat cross-legged, arms folded and tight-lipped, thinking about how late she was going to be for work again, fourth time in two weeks. Since Maxwell had designated himself manager in the absence of his mother at the Stop Button, she had already gotten a verbal and a written warning, next was termination for persistent lateness. She had bitten her tongue on many occasions, and this was now wearing thin. She really didn't want to join the queue down the job centre but wasn't sure how long she could hold out before she gave Maxwell Taste a good verbal harangue.

Sensing the tension, Lolly gave Veronica a friendly hug. Freeing all the feel-good feelings, she cracked half a sad smile.

Veronica reached for her tissues as her shoulders slumped and she began to explain the events over the last couple of weeks.

"I've had to take him out of class every day last week for 30 minutes at a time; he seems a bit different. Has something else happened maybe? Something he hasn't told you?" Lolly asked.

Veronica looked broken, head down with a heavy weight on her shoulders the tears effortlessly flowed. Swallowing heavily, she wiped away tear, after tear.

"It's since his birthday party! I just see Short Skirt Sally outside, tried to give me some nonsense talk!" Lolly giggled; Veronica didn't know how funny she actually was at times.

"Just imagine sitting there in your little mad scientist outfit waiting! No sod turns up. It hurt him. I hurt for him, and from that day, it's like he's getting worse." Veronica recalled the hope dwindle in Ray's eyes as he waited by the front door, hopeful that every passing stranger was one of his school friends. The frown lines of misunderstood sadness that she saw in Ray's face that day was permanently ingrained in her mind.

"With the autism and Tourette's syndrome sometimes, these things peak at a certain age; I see it all the time; it might just have been a coincidence that it was his party," Lolly reasoned.

"He's saying really strange things. Things that aren't happening. Things that aren't there. I think he might be hallucinating. What am I going to do? Have you noticed anything strange at school? Anything at all?"

Lolly started piecing together an unravelling puzzle, pausing for thought, it was like a light bulb appeared above her head.

"Just between the people in this room?" she said excitedly.

Veronica made an obvious face; there was only them two in the room! She leant in puffy eyed and intrigued.

"It all makes so much sense now! I see now! You know me; I'm totally spiritually connected! I believe in crystal balls, alignments and seeing into the future. Mystic Meg was my idol growing up. And that Uri Geller Pwhor!" Lolly fantasised.

"Ray is the same. Ray is blessed with a spiritual gift; he's like a, a, a psychic! HE SEES THINGS! I'm telling you! I been thinking this for ages. I just couldn't put my finger on it," Lolly said thinking on her epiphany. Veronica looked puzzled and unenlightened.

"Have you gone dotty?" Veronica asked. Lolly laughed shaking her head. She rested two small hands on her thigh as she spoke slowly pronouncing every syllable.

"Vee, Ray guessed I was pregnant!" Lolly continued.

"YES! He asked me if I swallowed two magic beans, not one, TWO!"

"Huh?"

"SURPRISE! Only just twelve weeks, and it's twins! I was gonna tell everyone at dinner. Spoilt the surprise now, but hey!" Lolly said raising her fluffy eyebrows in elation.

"What the!" Veronica was in total shock; after a moment of stillness, she picked up her dropped jaw and squeezed Lolly's hands; they did a joint screech in perfect unison.

"We have got so much to talk about," Lolly insisted.

"I know, I got loads of clothes you can have, saved them just in case. We need to talk baby showers, double buggies, names. Two babies, I can't believe it! And Ray…" Veronica was brought back from her wondering thoughts.

"Talk to Ray, Vee. Only he knows the answers; we can only surmise," Lolly said solemnly.

"I will. I will. I just need the right time. I'm gonna be late. If I want to keep my job and my sanity, I better get going. Can you just explain those scratches? I can't cope with that wobble woman at the front office right now!"

Veronica left the school office more disorientated than when she walked in. She wondered if the world had gone mad. Lolly had always been a little bit alternative thinking, but this was too farfetched, had pregnancy made Lolly totally loopy? Was Ray having a meltdown; had there been an escape of noxious gas in the school? Or was she the one losing her mind?

Chapter Eight
Chalk and Carrots

Ray spent the afternoon with Lolly in social skills session, helping a few select students thinking about actions, behaviours and consequences (ABC). Ray learnt how bumblebees helped the world by making honey, squishing them would only end up with the world having no honey – he decided then and there to never to squish another bumblebee. Between walking from the garden room back to the classroom, Ray had already forgotten!

Hasnat didn't understand Ray, and Ray didn't understand Hasnat, yet their misunderstanding of one another helped them develop a friendship only they understood. Chattering at the table, Hasnat and Ray poked fun of the boy that made no secret of eating his boogers, Mark Stompleton. Ray felt he had one up on him; he at least wiped them under the table. At exactly the same time, dangerously close to lunchtime, they felt peckish, both boys wondered what it was like to eat a booger. Maybe they'd give it a try, or maybe whilst there were no available boogers, they could eat something else, a bit of chalk Hasnat thought. Small bitesize, gravelly consistency he thought, not that dissimilar. Mrs Mayover always had some floating around her desk.

Hatching a what they thought was an ingeniously devious plan, Hasnat would distract the teacher, whilst Ray would get two pieces of chalk, crush it quickly and then they would both chomp it down when nobody was looking.

Hasnat tipped back and forth on his chair, rocking harder and harder until he exaggerated a big theatrical fall landing on his back like a turtle, legs and arms flailing; Hasnat pretended to cry.

"Oh heavens!" Miss Mayover cried as she hobbled over to Hasnat.

Ray seized the moment; he ran to her desk and begin to diver around. Nothing on the desk, maybe inside he thought. He rummaged so quickly through the draw he had almost forgotten what he was looking for.

"Ah ha!" Ray said quietly as he pocketed some colourful chalk. He was distracted from his mission when he saw a shiny mobile phone dazzling in the bottom of the draw. The lock screen hopped with bunny rabbits. Ray couldn't help it; the temptation got the better of him; he picked up the phone and began vigorously tapping at the bunnies; they ravished the screen as his finger resembled a juicy carrot.

"Ray!" Mrs Mayover yelled. Startled, his hands clumsily let go of the phone. It propelled into the air. He caught it. Dropped it. Then caught it again before it tumbled in slow motion; they both watched it fall across the desk onto the floor.

CRACK! Mrs Mayover closed her eyes in fury.

"What were you doing in my desk, Raymond Vision?" Mrs Mayover asked, her underbite protruding with anger. Ray started panicking, his hands unconsciously clenched, his head jarringly hitting his shoulder; he stuttered under the stress.

"We – we – we, was stealing…" He was unable to finish his sentence before he was interrupted.

"STEALING? My Phone! How could you?" she exclaimed.

The entire class uniformly gasped astounded at the revelation, and the furiousness of which they'd never heard of in Mrs Mayover's tone. Stealing was punishable by detention or exclusion she made sure everyone knew it! Pointing to the door, she demanded he leave.

"Straight to the head teacher!"

Ray was petrified he could not get out another word; he had once again been misunderstood and not allowed to speak. Now he was consumed with anger, fear and confusion; it was all whirling around in his head. He felt dizzy as his thoughts trailed off. Squishing as many bumblebees as he could, or not, he couldn't remember. He was confused.

Calling over to a passing teacher, she instructed him to watch her class.

Mrs Mayover pounded on the head teacher's wooden door before they were summoned in.

"Come in!" Mr Went bellowed, annoyed at the ferociousness of the door knock. Sat behind a neatly organised desk was a tall slender man. His face was hidden by a black beard, complimented by a push broom moustache with bristles of silver, his retreating hair line was shamefully obvious; he spoke with a soothing monotone voice, which immediately put people at ease.

Ray was visibly upset; he kept his head down and his mouth shut. Mrs Mayover ploughed straight in with her version of the event.

"I was administering first aid to a helpless student, sir, when this young boy out of nowhere went straight into my draw to STEAL my phone, breaking it in the process! Fact! He told me so," she continued, her voice high pitched and full of conviction. Ray could barely speak his hand tics out of control. Chin hitting his chest violently.

Mr Went asked unassumingly, "Is this true, Ray?" Ray shook his head in disagreement, as he opened his mouth, Mrs Mayover abruptly cut him off.

"He's a liar, sir!" She held up a cracked screen of distorted bunnies as evidence. Ray absorbed the anger exuberating from Mrs Mayover. He took a deep breath before he felt the uncontrollable warmth trickle down his trouser legs. Ray looked down in embarrassment as Mrs Mayover gasped in disgust.

"He's done that on purpose," she said tutting. Ray cupped his face in his hands and began to cry. Mr Went pointed towards the scowling teacher.

"Mrs Mayover, leave. I will speak with you later," he said sternly as he waved her out the room. Mr Went rested a big hand on his little shoulder.

"Don't worry about a thing, we are going to get you changed out of those wet trousers, get you a little snack, have a glass of water, a little calm down, and then you can come back here and we can talk about exactly what happened over a game of connect four, how does that sound?" Mr Went asked pointing to the games on his desk. Ray only heard connect four, his sniffles began to subside.

"Well done!" he praised.

Pressing the intercom, he called for Mrs Wiggle and Becky the midday assistant, to get Ray a fresh pair of trousers.

Moments later, they appeared at the door, Becky holding out a caring hand beckoned him over; he warily complied.

"I'll set this game up for when you get back." Mr Went smiled. Ray nodded.

After a fresh change of clothes, some warm cake and custard, Ray happily went back into Mr Went's office, a much more relaxed, slightly sheepish Ray walked in.

"Milk?" Mr Went asked offering him a little carton.

"Is it cold milk? Cause it's better for your bones; when it gets hot, you make the good bits disappear," Ray replied. Mr Went agreed, his children never ceased to amaze him.

"I'm red," Ray quickly decided before he guzzled down the milk.

"Before we play, there is one rule of this game. When we each put ONE counter in, we get to ask each other any question we like. You picked the colour. So, I'll go first!" he said. Ray agreed; he nodded a get on with it nod. Mr Went clunked a black counter in the middle slot.

"Do you sometimes have a sneaky sweet at home when your mum's not looking?" Mr Went asked. Ray laughed. He nodded in affirmation.

"Me too. When my wife goes to bed, I eat chocolate biscuits," Mr Went admitted. Ray put a red token in. He thought for a long moment.

"Do you hide secrets in your moustache, maybe sweets or stuff?" Ray said peering into his moustache. Mr Went let out a belly laugh.

"The only thing I hide in here is my secret grey hairs; I tuck them in," Mr Went said still laughing, as he put in the next counter.

"What were you doing in Mrs Mayover's drawer?" he asked. Without hesitation, Ray answered distracted by the game.

"Looking for chalk! My question. Do teachers get to eat the leftover cake from lunch after school?" he said before putting in a counter as close as he could to his others. Mr Went nodded a solid YES. Ray gasped; he knew it!

Adding another counter, Mr Went asked, "Did you take Mrs Mayover's phone?"

Ray answered quickly, "Nope! The rabbit bunnies on screen hopped up; they ate my finger cause they thought it was a carrot; Mrs Mayover shouted, and then I just dropped it by accident…Do you believe me?" Ray asked getting nervous. Mr Went nodded. Of course. He was proud of Ray, he had instinctive feelings for people that were telling the truth.

"100% I believe you, Ray!" Mr Went snuck in a question, followed by another.

"What were you going to do with the chalk?" Ray produced the chalk that he'd transferred from his wet trousers.

"I wanted to eat some with Hasnat; Mark was eating his boogers and we wanted to eat somethin'," Ray said with big truthful eyes. Mr Went wanted to let out a childish giggle; fully aware he was being watched, he held it back.

"Hasnat? I knew you two would get along! Well done, Ray! You have been very honest with me and hashed me at connect four!" This was too good to be true Ray thought, games, cakes and missing math.

"But…" Ray knew it.

"You and Hasnat will miss afternoon break time JUST for today for taking the chalk and conspiring to take the chalk and only the chalk, not the phone. I will speak with Mrs Mayover, and when she comes into class, she will be happy. She will not speak a word of this to you again! ANY problems, you come directly back to me; I don't care if you have to walk out of class, just come straight to me. No detours! I will sort it," Mr Went warned as he promised earnestly, handing him a hallway pass. Ray nodded notably less worried than before.

The boys stayed in Mr Raji's year six class all lunchtime watching the sunlight as it hit the monkey bars. It had never looked so appealing. They tidied up the reading books in the reading corner, put all the clean paint brushes in the pots for tomorrow morning and set out the afternoon's worksheet for Mr Raji who was enjoying a cup of coffee.

"I'm having a bad day!" Ray sighed.

"Me too! Oh, silly me! I forgot!" Hasnat exclaimed as he plundered into his pocket; he gave Ray a colourful party invite. Ray was tingling with excitement.

"It's gonna be THE BEST party! I want you to come; you can bring your mum too if you like," Hasnat said scratching at his raw skin splitting on his forearm. Ray ran over to the sink, got a wet paper towel and put it gently on Hasnat's arm. They smiled at each other; the day was bad but not as bad as it could have been.

Chapter Nine
Cat and Mouse

The week flew by, fortunately uneventful. Saturday had arrived, and Ray could barely contain his excitement. He clutched at the boxed present as they pulled up to Hasnat's gravel-covered driveway lined with potted palm trees and ornate ornaments; it was packed full of expensive cars.

Brimming over with enthusiasm, he flung open the car door leaving it flapping as he exploded towards the decorated front door. Veronica squinted bracing herself for a fall.

Balloons bobbed, and children ran crazily behind the frosted glass, the anticipation of someone answering the door was electric. Big smiles with welcome hugs paved the way to parents gingerly chatting whilst snacking on the party rings. A majority of the guests were Hasnat's extended family with the few exceptions from his old school; Ray was the only child from Red Wood Academy. A cloaked magician waved his wand wowing the children with disappearing coins and a mischievous appearing, disappearing white mouse named Jerry. Hasnat's mum bundled the family kitten under her arm when she caught him salivating over Jerry. Ushering the kitten safely in Hasnat's bedroom, she headed back downstairs to the party. The magician took a gallant bow; his performance was over. He would now work the room.

"Slushie time!" Hasnat's dad bellowed, screams of yay followed, while sugar-filled children made their way out into the conservatory. Ray awkwardly backed away; the urge to pee was overwhelming; not wanting another accident, he quickly slipped away unnoticed, as he went urgently looking for the bathroom. The house was huge it took him a while before he found the bathroom with one big toilet, and a strange little one beside it; he'd use the small one he decided.

Humming the happy birthday song whilst washing his hands, Ray happily flicked off the water, eager to get back to the children downstairs. Running wildly down the marbled hallway, Ray stumbled to his knees; pausing for thought, he heard the muffled 'Meow' with gentle scratching at a closed door along the landing.

Ray opened the door he was sure it came from very slowly. He was unsure of what he would find behind it; to his astoundment, he saw a beautiful Russian Blue kitten, eyes as big as saucers; it lovingly stared at him. It looked soft as a cloud. Ray embraced his new fluffy friend; he squeezed tighter and tighter.

To the kitten's relief, his attention was broken. Ray was dumbfounded by what stood before him; it was a bunkbed of dreams; it stood like a fortress in the middle of the room, solid and impenetrable! Built around the bed was a jungle gym, branches overreached with Hasnat's clothes hanging off and TWO tree trunk slides twizzled, joining the top of the bed all the way down to bottom foam map that resembled grass. He had to try it!

Scooting down the slide over and over, Ray screeched with glee; he wanted to try one last time and jump like an ogre from the top bunk. Jumping through the air, he let out a distinct roar; he landed heavily on an unsuspecting grooming kitten.

Fleeing from the stairs, Ray hid behind Veronica who was caught up in 'Grown up' conversation. Ray was too familiar with getting told off if he interrupted so he stayed quiet; she didn't notice him shielding himself behind her. A couple minutes past by when Hasnat's Aunt Cordelia appeared cradling a wailing, distressed, very injured cat.

Chapter Ten
St Thomas's

There was silence on the drive home. Ray's short-lived happiness had turned sour, like milk in the sun on a warm summer's day. He was blanketed with sadness; his lip quivered as he thought about his mum's face when Hasnat's mum had asked politely for everyone to leave.

Veronica was dying to ask the niggling question; it was trapped inside her, rumbling harder than a hunger pang; it needed to come out; she kept swallowing it back down and was afraid of the answer. She knew by the look on Ray's face he was somehow involved, but she needed to know either way.

Ray's chest was tightening; it was like a tourniquet around his torso; he began to hear his breath in his ears; it was like thunder crashing with every painful blink. All other sounds were being blocked out; he could hear his own heartbeat as he panted heavily; he struggled to catch his breath before letting out a loud gasp. The last thing Ray saw through heavy blinks was Veronica turn in fright, aghast she slammed on the brakes of the car; their bodies slumped to a halt before everything went black.

When Ray woke up groggily, his mum's dozing head rested on the hospital sheet that covered his legs.

Fainting from a serious panic attack, Ray was being kept under a watchful eye of the paediatric nurses at St Thomas's hospital in London. Veronica had not left his side; she was utterly exhausted from catching only a little doze in the hours after Ray had been admitted; she had teddy-tired eyes, her mouth was dry as a fossil, and her hair was unruly.

"Mum," he croaked; Veronica stroked back his hair.

"It's okay, my love, Mummy's here!" They hugged delicately as they embraced one another's familiar feel.

"I'm sorry," he whimpered full of remorse; Veronica shook her head gently.

"There is nothing we can't deal with. I promise. Whatever it is. Whatever you've done. Whatever is happening, I'm here! You need to start talking to me, please talk to me!" she pleaded. Ray widened his eyes in distress; he could see through the dampened chaos around him, the walls fizzled to transparency as his eyes adjusted to the environment; each area of focus melted away, layer by layer, every broken bone, ailment, condition, private moment and public interaction Ray could see.

A cracked skull.

Crotch scratching relief.

Dark shadows on shrivelled lungs.

A curled-up baby in a bulging belly.

Hugs and kisses, tears and fears.

People in toilets and their ablutions.

Doctors and nurses in resus trying desperately to save a frail limp body.

The pretenders, the hypochondriacs, attention seekers, the gravely ill, real pain, sufferance and hope, nothing was off limits even the odd miracle; Ray could see it all, and it bothered him.

"I can see EVERYTHING." Ray sighed.

"You can see everything?" she asked doubtfully; Ray nodded a big single yes.

He pointed to the next cubicle.

"On this side, there is a baby with a pink blankie; she has a turned around tummy. On that side, the bigger boy has five sewing things on his head," Ray said holding his breath waiting for a reaction; Veronica stepped back.

"What?" she questioned.

Ray stayed silent. Veronica thought he was pulling her leg; in disbelief, she slipped out of the cubicle. Veronica peered cautiously through the privacy of the adjacent floppy blue curtain. An overly engorged teenage boy spilled out the gaps in the chair as he viscously thumbed his PSP, while his mum took a picture of his stitches for her social media update. Veronica glanced back through Ray's curtain; his eyes were wide open, darting from side to side taking in the surroundings. Sheepishly, she shimmied across to the other cubicle, a flash of the pink blanket was enough. Veronica felt the butterflies fluttering widely in her stomach; the air now stifled her; she made a mad dash for an emergency exit at the end of the corridor. She lent on her knees to take deep breaths of fresh air before she could go back into the hospital. What was going on!

The baby swaddled in the knitted pink blanket lay in her dad's arms as he paced the sterile corridor. Veronica awkwardly loitered trying to catch a peek of the baby.

Crossing her arms, she pretended to read the wall posters, waiting before she pounced on the backward baseball cap-wearing, concerned young dad.

"She's beautiful," Veronica said no louder than a whisper.

He forced a strained smile on his tired face before she blurted out, "What's wrong with her?" Veronica asked.

"Erm, it's called volvulus. It's a VERY serious condition. She's going to surgery, like now, now!" he said frown lines almost covering his eyebrows; he shook his head still in disbelief at the diagnosis. Veronica began to edge away, full of genuine hopefulness for the babe in arms.

She said, "I hope she gets well soon." Slipping back into Ray's confined cubicle, she whipped out her phone, googling volvulus she felt her own stomach knot as the pages struggled to load.

"Twisted!" she read aloud. She held her breath as she digested the words. The truth was much harder to swallow than she had expected. The silence between Veronica and Ray had never seemed so loud.

Dr Patrick sprung back the flappy curtain grinning inanely, startling both Ray and Veronica. He read aloud the medical chart. Ray squirmed awkwardly as the tall man towered over him talking gibberish.

"You are doing excellent, Master Vision. Just excellent!" he praised; his tight animal print shirt that was too small, it popped at the buttons revealing a peek of a hairy belly; it made the animals stretch, looking a lot bigger than normal.

"Can we go home now, doctor?" Veronica asked exhausted.

"You sure can! You sure can! I will just give you the discharge papers, and you'll be on your merry way. Any concerns, high temperature, headaches, dizziness, abnormal breathing bring him straight back. Couple days off school as well, young man. Some much-needed rest and relaxation is the best medicine!" Dr Patrick handed over a scrap of paperwork; patting Veronica gingerly on the back, he waved a sassy goodbye.

Veronica slowly packed away Ray's belongings in his overnight dragon-shaped bag.

"I'm sorry, Mummy," Ray murmured. Veronica pulled Ray close to her chest, nestling her head in his hair.

"I just couldn't explain it; it was harder than mouse cheese. It's my brain again, and I couldn't say why my eyes don't see normal stuff!" Ray said raising his eyebrows. Doe-eyed he looked up at Veronica; she gave a comforting nod. All Veronica wanted now was the hug she was getting; she needed it. They both did.

"I want you to see what my eyes see," Ray said.

"I do too." She smiled.

Chapter Eleven
Last Orders

Laying uncomfortably on her bed, Mrs Taste peered through her thick-rimmed glasses at the wad of orders that she had received over the weekend. One in particular required urgent attention. A Saudi Arabian princess was having a royal engagement; her personal designer was making a bespoke outfit to match her high-heeled shoes. The flamboyant designer required some unique buttons to go on a chic embroidered jacket and buttons to finish off the pointy toe pair of heels. Each mother of pearl button needed to be carefully etched with a dove in flight. The job was to be completed and shipped within three working days, with a large bonus if they arrived earlier.

As she was debating what she was going to do with all of the work piling up, she heard the door creak; she was well aware that her son Maxwell was on the creep. Over the weekend, she had noticed that money was disappearing from her purse. At first, it was a £5 note, and gradually as the weekend had passed by, she was missing upwards of £100 pounds. Only Maxwell was in the house, and she had her sneaking suspicions that he had been helping himself to her money for some time now. Stern faced and ready for a confrontation, she waited for him to skulk into her room.

Maxwell's scraggy hair made an appearance before he did. Startled that she was waiting for him, he burst awkwardly into the room. His eyes unable to keep off her purse, he began to fumble his words.

"What you doin' up, Mum?" he asked faking concern. He reached to adjust her pillows before she let out a vicious swipe, forcing him to retreat.

"Vhat are you doing up, Maxwell?" She threw back the question, turning out her empty purse. Maxwell didn't look surprised; he was shocked she had dared to bring the subject up.

"So?" he asked nonchalantly.

"So, you took my money, without my permission!" Mrs Taste asked thinking about all the other missing bits of money she had chalked up to her forgetfulness. Maxwell had an answer for everything.

"You were asleep! You would have given it if you was awake, so what's the problem?" he asked not caring what the answer was. Mrs Taste pelted Maxwell with one insult after the other; his blank stare let her know he couldn't be less interested; he stopped her mid-sentence.

"Listen, I should've, would've, could've but didn't. It's done; let's stop going on about it." Maxwell looked bored now.

"Stop going on? You took advantage when I woz asleep!" she continued; he interrupted with a nasty laugh.

"All those women at work take advantage of you! The minute your back's turned, they're skiving off down the café, laughing at you whilst they're getting paid for working, they're the ones taking your money! Taking it down the pub! You don't say anything about that, do you! Pathetic!" he said spitefully. Mrs Taste stayed silent in shock at the outrageous back chat. She was quietly livid as Maxwell laughed at her before he walked out the room slamming her bedroom door. She stewed for long moments on his words.

Still shaken from her recent fall, her body still ached, and her hands were still unsteady; they shook even more now with anger; she quickly busied her mind with her work. The royal engagement would take her mind to where it was most happy at 'The Stop Button'; she knew she was not up to the job but knew a woman that was. Veronica's talent and precise engraving skills would be a perfect match for the job; she was always willing to work overtime and was fully aware the extra cash came in handy.

Using her rolodex, she found the number she was looking for. Placing her finger in the old dial phone face, she turned it clockwise with each number she dialled; she called Veronica at home.

"Gut morning, Veronica, Mrs Taste here," she said gazing over the order in her hand.

"Hello, Mrs Taste, I was just going to call you," Veronica began.

"Apologies for calling on a Sunday evening. I have a most important assignment! I will pay handsomely if you can finish z job. It's for an Arabian Princess," Mrs Taste voice was high, overjoyed at the prospect of getting the job; it was such an honour to have royal jobs, which were few and far between. The Stop Button always received news coverage from a royal event which boosted business interest. Veronica paused, swallowing her fear as she spoke.

"Mrs Taste, Ray and I have just got home from the hospital; I'm exhausted and—" Veronica was interrupted.

"Ohhhh! Are you both okay?" she screeched wincing in pain as she jerked her back awkwardly forwards.

"We're both fine. But Ray needs time off school, so I need time off work. The whole week. I wouldn't normally ask at such short notice, but it really can't be helped," Veronica said nervously, not wanting to disappoint Mrs Taste.

"Nonsense! Bring him with you to z shop. He can help me; we can make strawberry lemonade; he can sort through the buttons; we will have gut fun!" she said optimistically anticipating she would return to work.

"No. This time I really can't! I'm really sorry; I need to spend some time with my son; there are things we have to do. I can't explain everything right now; I don't even understand. I just need to take the week off." Veronica affirmed to herself she was doing the right thing. Mrs Taste tut-tutted in annoyance; she was already having a very bad morning, and this just topped it all off; she could not believe the disloyalty after everything she had excused her for recently, days off, medical appointments, sick days and now when she truly needed her she was taking a week off; she felt betrayed, almost like Veronica was taking 'advantage'.

"Veronica Vision. I will not be taken advantage of anymore! If you do not come to work, you give me no choice, I will have to fire you with immediate effect!" Mrs Taste scorned as she had an instant bitter taste in her mouth from the harsh acidic words she had delivered. Neither spoke for a few awkward moments. Veronica thought carefully.

Taking advantage? She remembered someone else saying that not too long ago.

"Well, Mrs Taste, Ray comes first, and I will have to respectfully decline your offer," Veronica said near to tears.

"Nein problem! I will get your last payslip in z post. We have no further conversation." Mrs Taste abruptly hung up the telephone leaving Veronica gobsmacked. Immediately regretting listening to the idiotic ramblings of her son, what was done, was done, a proud woman she couldn't take it back now, the long peaceful working relationship meant nothing she stubbornly told herself as she shed an angry tear.

Chapter Twelve
Late Night Trolling

Veronica had taken up a spot in the middle of a rug. Sitting in every yoga pose she could achieve, she manically wore out her search engine. The internet was running slow with all the devices she was working off at the same time. iPad resting on the coffee table, laptop between her legs, mobile phone leant up the chair leg and Kindle hidden under some magazine articles.

Surrounded by store-bought books, borrowed books, library lends, e-books, research papers and healthcare pamphlets that covered the entire floor, Veronica searched for answers; this time in different places. She brought out every baby book, photograph, picture Ray had drawn, finger painting, hand mould he'd made, certificate and class achievement he had crafted from the day he was born; she kept them all in a golden box ready for when he was old enough; she had collected so many things she'd forgotten half of them existed.

With her burning eyes and adrenaline running from the caffeine, she googled and binged everything from high-functioning autism to Samson's hair being the source of his strength.

Trolling through paranormal events, she came across a ghoulish website of haunted London. It was more haunted than she'd ever considered, a picture caught Veronica's eye. The theatre that her and Ray had visited only a few weeks earlier was believed to have been built on a plague pit from the 1600s. Bones had been excavated in the 1980s when it was built – however, work had halted as there was an overwhelming desire to get the theatre built as quickly as possible to keep the investors happy. Veronica felt a chill travel the entire length of her spine. Dead people in the floor, dusty old bones; it all made so much sense. Poor Ray, if only everyone knew, she contemplated.

Desperately reading blogs and Tumblr, she glanced at the clock; it read just after 1 am. Veronica was about to call it a night, when a title caught her blurry eyes.

'Light is to darkness what love is to fear in the presence of one the other disappears.'

Veronica laughed as she had a familiar realisation, keeping it simple was always best. When Veronica was a young girl, her mother had always told her she was complicated, and that simplicity was the key to a quiet, successful life. Now she saw things with a new clarity. She hatched a plan.

She just hoped that her idea would work.

Chapter Thirteen
The Thames

Ray sat on the jubilee line with his musical ear defenders, and Veronica's trendy black sunglasses balancing on his fishing hat, oblivious to the analytical adults. The train rocked back and forth down the tunnel as he swung his legs to the beat of the soothing music. That was the noise filtering out the way. One small step. Veronica gave herself an imaginary pat on the back.

Three stops left…

Veronica was putting the finishing touches on her job application for the local supermarket. She needed a job and quick.

Two stops left…

Ray still content looked at the interconnectedness of the train lines above their heads.

One stop left…

Tapping his knee, they got off the train at Westminster hand in hand. Veronica helped Ray straighten her wonky sunglasses that he had quickly flipped down; Ray's vision was obscured by the protective lenses.

Walking along the embankment, they stepped out onto Westminster Bridge. The midmorning breeze took their breath away as they battled the wayward wind. Stopping in the middle, they looked out on London Town. Tugboats sat idly, bobbing in the water. An emergency speedboat tore through the murky Thames River at breakneck speed. The sun hit the enormous buildings at an angle reflecting in the glum waves that crashed on the steep moss-ridden banks whilst few ducks milled around waiting for some scraps to be thrown over the sides. Ray gulped as he peered sceptically over the top of the sunglasses looking down the seemingly endless stretch of the river.

"Woah!" he gasped knocking the glasses clean off his face; he stepped back covering his eyes. Veronica put both arms around him.

"I'm here with you. Let us look together! What do you see?" Veronica gave Ray a reassuring squeeze. She slowly lowered his resisting hands.

"Too much stuff! Way too much old stuff! Big stuff! Tiny stuff, just stuff, stuff!" Ray said fearfully. Veronica brought out two drawing pads. Sitting down on the bridge, she began to draw on the paper; passers-by looked curiously as she plotted up on the pavement; they wondered if they were a pair of street performers. Veronica gently put the glasses back on Ray's face and pulled him down to her.

"When you're ready, just peep over the glasses. I'll draw what I see. No peaking at my picture till I'm finished! You can draw if you like too, up to you!" she said knowing he'd be unable to resist. Handing him some pencils, he was on board from the second he gripped the end of the pencil. Ray's love of art explained what he could not, and she had realised that last night when she was going through his golden box.

Ray sat as close to Veronica as he could get without sitting right in her lap.

Ray rotated and vigorously shaded; he re-rotated and held his picture up to the light and measured with his pencil; he angled the paper, completely immersed until the whole page was filled accurately down to the smallest detail. Ray's exceptional artistic talent despite being delayed in all other areas was impeccable; it far superseded that of an established artist. Veronica knew that this was his strength – his superpower; it was going to carry Ray in his life, and she would encourage him so far as he was happy to go. Art was different for Ray; this he clearly understood, colours, lighting and shadowing; this was simple; the pencil did the work; he was only the guide.

"3 – 2 – 1. Swap!" they said together.

Ray giggled at Veronica's attempt, stick men walked on the pavements, disproportionate clouds lined the sky, and shadows of trees were all in the wrong places making him laugh; he knew full well she was much better than she was making out. Veronica scanned Ray's picture carefully; immediately, she was impressed; his drawing was brilliant and so quickly done. On the surface, it just looked like a still image of exactly what they were looking at, but deeper into the drawing, it didn't paint the happy surface picture. The glistening sun-reflective river looked dicey and dangerous; everything drawn was perfectly replicated. What was captured beneath the water was mind blowing. It was home to shoals of fish and creepy critters. There were unmistakable mounds of mismatched bones scattered in the Thames, big ones, small ones, little skulls, big skulls, large unidentifiable animal bones and decaying fish bones. Wrecked ship debris bulged out of the mud only inches from the surface unnoticed by all. There were shiny little sparkles resembling coins scattered amongst the foliage that lay on the riverbed. A small collection of wardrobes and furniture had been dumped only a few yards from where they sat, slowly being torn apart by the current. Heavy-looking cement blocks with handcuffs lay idle at the bottom of the river, why was anyone's guess.

Veronica looked at Ray.

"These things here, Ray, you can see them right now?" Veronica asked. Ray nodded looking back out at the river over the glasses. Looking out at the river, she slowly pieced together that Ray could see through everything; he was like a little superhero, with powers; she kept this to herself; she didn't want him trying to fly off the bridge. He had vision like no other little boy, an 'X Ray Vision'; she gasped.

"You are amazing, Raymond! Don't ever be afraid of what you see. If you don't like it, just put on the glasses, or if there's no glasses, look away! It is just that simple, just don't look. I'm here now, and I understand. Mum understands," Veronica said promising to always look after him; she felt a relief lifted off her shoulders, a burden lifted as a new one developed. How to keep this a secret? They sat for long moments looking out at the slappy waves.

"Let's get some frozen yoghurt, and we'll carry on our adventure," Veronica said excitedly.

"Shrek Adventure? And bubble gum flavour yoghurt?" Ray asked, his face full of delight. Veronica couldn't resist.

"Sure, we can try Shrek if you want. And a big bubble gum yoghurt for my brave boy. Remember what I said. You got your ear defenders, our sunglasses and you got me, we're all here for you!" she said as they began their journey.

Sitting on the grass watching the contortionists perform, Ray made a sticky mess around his face with his yoghurt.

"So, do you see in colour or is it like black and white?" Veronica asked curiously, downplaying the phenomenal discovery as she baby-wiped his face vigorously.

"Yah! I do. The walls and stuff are like electric colour, and if you're behind it, I can see you. It goes like a Twizz and a Fizz! Then it's gone! See through! I can see inside and outside your body too, at the same time!" he added. Veronica didn't know how she felt about this. I mean clothes on or off she thought? Hopefully on! She daren't ask just yet.

By the end of the day, they had grown much closer than ever before.

They spent the rest of the week side by side embarking on a real journey of discovery.

Chapter Fourteen
Wiggly Wiggly

Ray was none too pleased about returning to the iron castle of Redwood Academy. It was all work, work, work; they didn't think about anything else in that place. He was dreading seeing Hasnat for the first time since the kitten breaking his leg fiasco.

Veronica sat down in the sensory office, with a beaming smile while Ray was equally excited; his mood mimicked his mum's; they both looked at burst point. Lolly was so happy to see them so happy; it was such a welcome change as of lately things were so serious in this room.

Ray sprawled over the bean bags watching the bubbly fish tubes, as Veronica confided in Lolly.

"Lorraine, you remember we had that conversation about Ray having a gift?" Veronica asked in full agreement of her own question. Lolly nodded enthusiastically, full of exuberance as she waited for the revelation as Veronica whispered adding to the drama.

"It's true! Every single word of it! He's a genius." She laughed manically. Lolly grinned a confused smile; she knew Veronica didn't believe in all that stuff.

"Explain," Lolly urged.

"Tell Auntie Lorraine. Sorry we're at school. Tell Lolly," Veronica instructed Ray as she corrected herself. Upside down and the blood whooshing to his head, he took a moment to gather his words.

"I have X-RAY Vision!" He laughed. Veronica nodded in all seriousness. That was it, both mother and child were conspiring, likely they were having a joke knowing how gullible she was.

"We're not crazy!" Veronica said. Lolly was unaware of her own distorted and disgruntled face.

"NO?" Lolly asked.

"I know it sounds insane! He really does! How did he know you were pregnant?" Veronica insisted.

"Educated guess?" Lolly questioned.

"Educated in that subject? Ray? No chance! He still believes he was delivered by the stork on the doorstep in a swaddle," Veronica whispered.

"Well, it's obviously his X-Ray eyes! How could I have missed it!" Lolly said sarcastically. Veronica rolled her eyes at her oldest friend, the most un-sceptical person she knew, was being sceptical. Drastic measures were needed to convince Lolly. Veronica pointed to the opposite side of the room.

"I mean..., I'm there saying psychic, and you've come up with X RAY eyes! Now who's gone dotty?" Lolly insisted.

"Ray, that wall there? What's behind it?" Veronica asked.

"That's Mr Went's office," Lolly replied. Ray glanced over at the wall; teetering his head from side to side, he took a flash picture in his memory before shutting his eyes.

"Was it bad?" Veronica questioned.

"Not bad! Just yucky! Mr Went and Mrs Wiggle are having some mouth cuddles," Ray said in disgust. Both adults gasped covering their mouths. Holding back an inane smirk, Veronica beckoned Lolly to go look; she half reluctantly left the room.

Contemplating knocking, Lolly decided against it, entering abruptly. There was a mad dash when the door swung open, wet lips were wiped, and Mrs Wiggles fixed her ruffled hair. Mr Went's untucked shirt didn't go a miss. They both looked a pale shade of 'just got caught in the act'. Lolly could finally envision after all these years what a deer in headlights looked like. This was it. Deer's plural she surmised.

"I'm sorry, sir, I just wanted a moment, but I can see you're having one already." Without waiting for a reply, she slammed the door shut.

Skulking back to the sensory office biting her lip, she shot Veronica a look of bemusement before holding her stomach in laughter.

"Scan-de-los!" she cried as her and Veronica roared with laughter. Composing herself, she sat opposite Ray on the bean bag.

"You saw all that, Ray?" Lolly asked astounded looking at Ray like she had never seen him before. He nodded overjoyed; Lolly appeared delighted.

"You are EXTRAORDINARY! Vee this is unheard of, you know that right?" Lolly flopped on the bean bag with Ray looking for a tickle spot.

"Wowww!" Lolly was choked. Pausing for thought she put her hands on her growing tummy.

"Can you see my babies?" Lolly asked, her eyes widen in excitement. Ray nodded and glanced at her baby pouch.

"They look funny, like floating beans with teeny, tiny arms; I think their playing." He laughed. Lolly's eyes surged with tears as she squeezed Ray who didn't do hugs too well; he only tolerated them even from his mum.

"He has a gift!" Lolly whispered.

"It was on his birthday. He said it came from the stars, from up above," Veronica whispered half disbelievingly, half not knowing what was possible anymore.

"Just woke up that day, and poof, it was there, but it wasn't there the day before," Veronica explained; the astonishment she had initially felt was still as vibrant as the first moment she realised.

"We need to talk this out; something like this could be of big interest to…" Lolly could not find the words to encapsulate the phenomenon.

"The world, I know. We have to protect him. Let's talk tonight," Veronica replied. The seriousness between the two was clear.

Chapter Fifteen
The Fish Counter

Veronica felt like a fish doctor in her white pressed coat and covered hair, all she needed was a stethoscope. It was her first day on the job, and she was trying to embrace her new position as fish counter operative. Posh word for smelly fishmonger she thought. She wore proudly on her face a big professional smile as she failed to notice the five-day old sardine that had been maliciously placed in the lining of her collar, wafting a rank fishy smell wherever she walked.

Out of nowhere, a freakishly thin, tall, strawberry blonde haired, wirey mismatched ginger bearded 22-year-old man appeared at the counter with an arrogant lean.

"I'm Dave, your new supervisor – yeh. So, erm, you're the trainee – yeh. Never had a trainee before! Ever gut a fish? Deboned? Descaled? Cut a darne of salmon?" Unimpressed, he threw the glass cleaning liquid over to Veronica; she caught it like a ninja.

"You get the counters sparklin, the glass gleamin, and I'll get you a fish. Hope you're not squeamish." He laughed.

Veronica sighed; she meticulously cleaned down the display cabinets; they obviously had not seen a deep clean in a while. She carefully aligned the poorly displayed fish and tidied up the fish counter; she mocked Dave by arrogantly leaning on the counter waiting for further instructions.

"Newbie!" Dave called. Veronica watched as Dave expertly gutted a fish from the belly downwardly; he flicked out the insides; they landed a millimetre away from her. Dave handed her a bendy knife; Veronica apprehensively took it from his hand. Her steady hand from all the years of engraving buttons, glided the knife through the fish like a hot knife through butter; Dave was gutted; she was so good.

"I got this, Dave, can't be rocket science right?!" She laughed.

"Just make sure you cut and prep on the blue boards! Let me know when you finished; I got plenty more jobs for you." He deliberately misaligned her display case she had just arranged before he sauntered off. Dave was intimidated; the newbie would be a manager in no time; he silently panicked.

Veronica was determined to do a good job; she would be the best fish Counteress she could be. She giggled quietly to herself.

"Counteress, I'll be the manageress soon," she said.

After a few weeks, Veronica was getting the hang of the job. Knowing the routine was a snip, and she was starting to become a bit of a fish connoisseur; she could tell a kipper from a mackerel just by the waft from the closed boxes. She woke up every day and dreaded going to a job she hated. She'd look at Ray's face in the mornings and remind herself why she was doing what she was doing. That made the days bearable, and the short hours made the days tolerable. Dave had become ever cockier; he was more of a dictator than a boss.

"The fish demand better gutting – the surveillance camera caught you coming back 30 seconds late from lunch!! Only one of us is allowed a 45-minute break and it's not you," he'd spiel.

Veronica was on her lunch break; she sat, took off her jacket in the locker room placing it on the bench next to her – another sardine fell out her collar. Dave's little joke was wearing thin. She picked up a folded newspaper and began reading it.

The newspaper headlines stopped her dead in her tracks.

'Husband to appear at magistrates court for double murder.'

Veronica carried on reading. Every word made her even more anxious than the last. Brutal. Savage. Knife. Stomach. Relentless. Unforgiving. Postman killed as he caught the perpetrator trying to dispose of the body; it was gripping stuff, the words jumping out of the page at her. What's more, it became apparent that it was the corner house where she and Ray had the car accident. She knew then that Ray had seen it. He had seen it all, and he was a witness. An unreliable one, but a witness nonetheless. She could just see it now; the day in court.

"And how did you see the event, Mr Vision?" the barrister would ask.

"Oh, I saw it with my X Ray eyes," Ray would answer with Jeff the dragon at his side. Comical to say the least, she laughed as she stared off into the distance. Poor woman, she thought. Poor Ray. Just then she caught a whiff of herself, poor me, she sighed.

Chapter Sixteen
Missing

Veronica was taking Ray to the local shop; she bargained a vigorous walk up the hill to the corner shop in return for a sweet treat.

Ray swung like a chimpanzee from lamppost to lamppost, waiting for Veronica to safely wave him onto the next. He suddenly froze, his eyes wandering over a missing poster. Looking sadly into the ginger cat's bright green snake, slit eyes, he pulled a sour face – he read aloud.

'Missing Ginger cat Ronald, polka dot collar and stumpy tail, last seen on Wellington Avenue. Reward for safe return.'

"I can make it right if I help another kitty, Mum," Ray said, full of remorse for injuring his friend Hasnat's kitten.

"How can you help?" Veronica reluctantly asked, hoping it wouldn't end with them walking the streets.

"We can look! I can look, look! I can see, oh please, please, please!" he pleaded, Veronica sighed deeply.

"We'll see," she replied.

After a word every mouthful at dinner, a film Veronica never got to watch and a long drawn-out bedtime story, she finally gave in.

"Ray, if I promise to take you to look for the cat first thing in the morning, will you PLEASE stop talking?" she now pleaded. Ray nodded energetically. Tucking in each side in turn, she gave him a squeeze before heading off to bed.

"Jeff!" he yelled. She returned to give Jeff his kiss on the nose.

Morning came earlier than Veronica had hoped. Ray shimmied on the floor like an uncontrollable, wiggly worm; he waited for a short moment before pouncing onto her bed, frightening her awake out of her peaceful slumber. Collecting her thoughts, she glanced at Ray.

"Good morning to you too!" she said sarcastically as she ruffled his bed hair. He pulled out a magnifying glass; he was ready to play real detectives.

Eating his cereal bar, Ray impatiently huffed and puffed as he waited by the front door, rattling the handle. Veronica momentarily savoured the moment; every school day, it tended to be the other way around; it was bittersweet, and she knew tomorrow she would be doing the huffing. They briskly walked down a small pathway to the main road; Ray whispered to his assistant Detective, Major, Lieutenant Jeff; agreeing with him, he said, "We need to trace the paw steps!" he mimicked Jeff's Scottish accent. Veronica chuckled at the dragon's intuition; they led the way with Ray's handy magnifying glass; Veronica behind, carefully looking for paw prints.

Two hours later and four bottles of water drunk, they still roamed the nearby streets. Looking in front gardens and cautiously peering over back gardens, Ray had seen everything from people playing twister in their living rooms, family mealtimes, to bath time frolics. He was getting tired of looking. Just as things were looking bleak, and there was no sign of a missing cat, the detective trio began retracing their own steps. Ray saw a small winding road that they had not yet ventured down; tugging on Veronica's sleeve, she reluctantly followed him down to a small allotment hidden by dense trees.

Overgrown bushes and shrubbery spread far across the open field; varieties of vegetables grew freely in neat little private fenced plots, whilst ripened fruits fell from small fig trees. Rickety sheds and mossy green houses were scattered through numerous patches. They slowly walked through the allotment amongst the entwined, prickly blackberry bushes.

Ray pointed at a wooden shed on the other side of the allotment. He jumped up and down.

"What is it?" Veronica asked. Ray could barely breathe; he just kept pointing frantically. Grabbing Ray's hand, they whisked their way through the budding growth.

"In here?" Veronica asked looking through the frosted shed window. There was a weather-worn, handwritten note nailed on the door.

'Back in a week, Bob, don't forget to water my pumpkins.

And keep an eye on those pesky slugs.'

The owner was away, and the door was locked. Veronica could see the cat curled up in a plant pot.

"Sleeping!" Ray said. Veronica gulped; she hoped he was sleeping. She looked for something to break the window, until she spied a flimsy padlock.

"Oh, no, Kitty's stuck FOREVER!" Ray cried near to tears. Scanning the near empty plot, she saw a rusty spade resting on a fence panel.

Veronica gave Ray a disapproving look of her imminent actions; he grinned at his mum's rebellion. One powerful swipe later, she had knocked off a jagged piece of wood from the doorframe, padlock and all. Opening the creaking door, they peeped inside. In the corner of the shed was a startled ginger cat with a polka dot collar, stump of a tail and big scared saucer eyes. Ron was thin from not eating, but luck was on his side, a split water butt filled with bitty rainwater had kept him hydrated during his imprisonment.

"Be careful, he might get clawy!" Veronica jumped to shield Ray. Gently bending down, the cat flew into her arms for affection, butting his head on her face; she scooped him up. Hearts melting, they all walked across the allotment. Ray excitedly preoccupied when Veronica was smashing the lock had stomped the growing pumpkins; he pointed out his accident to Veronica on the way out. Mortified, she thought of the owner's face when they returned to a broken shed, cat leavings and pumpkin squash. She couldn't deal with it all at once. First thing was first, get Ronald home, deal with the shed issue later.

Tearfully overjoyed with the return of her precious boy, Patty, Ron's owner, showered Ray and Veronica with smelly, musty hugs emanating from her fuddy–duddy jumper. By way of gratitude, she pressed a small brown envelope reading 'Reward Money' into Veronica's hand; she refused to take the envelope.

"We don't want the money; it's not necessary," Veronica said. Patty handed the envelope to Ray who immediately beamed with delight.

"Ye'h can n ye'h will!" Patty demanded. They watched as Ron made himself back at home; his curious feline companions sniffing, wondering exactly where he had been for the last few days. Putting Ron in his basket next to one of his many brothers, they watched as they lovingly tussled with one another.

"I've got back me special boy, now go do somethin nice for yeselves," Patty said shutting the door on the kind strangers.

"She had a lot of cats," Ray said wafting away the smell; he began to open the envelope; seeing a flash of purple notes, he shrieked; Veronica pinched it shut. Ray shot her a grumpy look. As did Jeff.

"I have an idea," Veronica said.

Returning to the allotment, they carefully went back to the shed where they had found Ronald. Rummaging through her bag for her trusty pen, she wrote on the reward envelope 'Sorry' before laying it on the shelf in the shed. She wedged back the shed door securing it with the spade.

"Let's go get some doughnuts, detectives!" Veronica said.

Case closed.

Chapter Seventeen
Oh for Fish Sake!

A week had gone by at a slug's pace. Veronica had gutted countless fishes and shovelled tons of ice in and out of the display units, whilst Dave the supervisor, supervised. The permanent smell of fish she was sure was stained on her skin; people twitched their nose when she was around and avoided her in the locker room; the looks were blatantly obvious, she stunk, and she knew it!

Serving a customer, she watched Dave gossiping childishly to a giggly teenage girl in the aisle who looked a lot older than she actually was; she sighed as she had slogged not only the fish's guts out but her own. Veronica was fed up; this job was not for her; she had tried, she really had, but it was soul destroying. Veronica was creative and bubbly; this job was flat and bleak. She desperately missed the banter of her work colleagues in The Stop Button, the familiar chugging of the conveyer belt and her own little creative tea-stained drawing board.

Joining every recruitment site she could find, she handed out piles of virtual CVs and filled out endless application forms. Not so much as a shortlisting. It felt hopeless. For now, she was going to have to stick it out, if she wanted to pay her bills.

Washing her hands for the umpteenth time in the hand basin, a clatter of keys on the counter and a phlegmy cough caught her attention; attentively, she came over to serve the customer.

"Can I he—?" Veronica began as she blinked upwardly, pausing at Mrs Taste who was smiling sorrowfully. Both stood their ground, wishing the other to break the silence first. Mrs Taste eventually wavered.

"Can I have that lonely looking red mullet over zere? I think it may need to come back with me to my shop," Mrs Taste insinuated motioning to a fish in the display.

"That red mullet isn't lonely; it has plenty of other fish in the unit keeping it company! Perhaps for yourself this snapper would be more appropriate?" Veronica said sarcastically.

"Misunderstood creatures I'm sure! I heard they only snap when dey are extremely stressed," Mrs Taste answered.

"The red mullet will never feel safe with the snapper around, the stability of her ecosystem is what's most important," Veronica stated. Mrs Taste shook her head dramatically.

"Oh, CAN z fish talk! I vant you to come back! Can you forgive my harshness?" she respectfully asked. Veronica stubbornly shook her head.

"No," she said reluctantly.

Mrs Taste took a deep breath, saddened by the two-letter word. She expected nothing more from the woman that reminded her of herself.

"A proud woman you are, Veronica Vision. Dis is a big shame. Vhat to do?" Mrs Taste looked around aimlessly as Veronica awkwardly played with the fish in the display.

"Okay. I vish you vell," Mrs Taste said as she walked away, a walking stick steading her stride. Regrettably, Veronica watched her leave; she thought she'd make a bit more of an effort. Realising she had left the keys on the counter, Veronica chased after her.

"YOUR KEYS! MRS TASTE, YOUR KEYS!" Veronica called after her. Unfazed, she turned.

"Nein! They're not mine! They're my new manager's keys. The person that will inherit my beloved Stop Button after I have retired. The person who loves my business just as much as I do, dat's who those keys belong to." Mrs Taste shook her head certain she had made the right choice.

"Dat person will slowly buy me out of z business. I will receive a small percentage of z yearly profit until I am no longer z owner; they will make sure it grows from strength to strength!" Tingles flew down Veronica's spine as Mrs Taste continued.

"This person puts their family first and is z most trustworthy. Can you see she gets dem?" Mrs Taste held her hands behind her back refusing to take back the keys. Veronica utterly shocked stared thoughtfully at the keys, her dream job in her hand; she held them like dainty glass. As Veronica went to speak a word, Mrs Taste was hobbling halfway down the aisle.

"Must dash! See you Saturday bright and early." Mrs Taste waved her handkerchief over her shoulder.

A smile creeped onto Veronica's face; elated, she took off her jacket and ripped through her hairnet.

Dave was leant over a different girl than before in the adjacent aisle admiring her slick blonde hair and trying to catch a peek down her blouse.

"So, I got a big boy's Mustang; we can go for a ride at the weekend if you're nice to me!" he bragged. Veronica tapped Dave on the shoulder, placing her jacket and remanence of her hairnet in his hands; she shook her head at him pitifully.

"He doesn't have a Mustang, sweetheart; he has a Ford Escort with broken electric windows that he borrows from his nan," Veronica said bluntly. Dave began to stutter as the girl laughed at his shame.

"I quit." She smiled. Veronica walked away leaving Dave speechless; he fumbled as he tried to explain his lie. Veronica returned; putting a sardine in his top pocket, she squished it against his chest and smiled childishly.

"And you forgot this!"

Veronica walked away as if springs were in the souls of her shoes, throwing in the air and catching the keys to The Stop Button.

Chapter Eighteen
Silver Linings

Ray was trying his hardest to impress the bigger boys in the playground; they just kept laughing. His kick-up skills were not as impressive as he thought; his mum thought they were amazing, what was their problem? After not getting much attention that he was desperately craving, Ray gradually gravitated to a lonesome corner with his ball.

Kicking the ball against the wall, he drowned out the sound of the playground screams of fun and laughter.

"Can I play football with you?" a voice asked. Ray nodded, his head almost falling off with enthusiasm. It was Hasnat.

They played together awkwardly silent, yet blissfully happy to be in one another's company again. Ray eventually blurted out what was on both their minds.

"I' m sorry about your little cat!"

"My mum said it was just a terrible accident; she said there is a bright side to every line that's silver, and when he was at the vet, he got something removed that he didn't need, and now, he doesn't do pee pees in the house all the time, so it's actually good," Hasnat said, pleased with the outcome. Ray smiled as Hasnat plodded along with the conversation not fully taking in every word, just the sound of his voice was enough.

"So, Ray, I been thinking. Since I moved to London, I don't have like a best friend anymore, and well, I need one. Do you want to be it?" Hasnat asked openly. Ray didn't give him a chance to finish his sentence; he agreed leaping onto Hasnat to hug him; they momentarily embraced the hug before Hasnat shrug him off quickly.

"We can't do hugs. People will call us boyfriend and boyfriend!" Hasnat said looking around the playground; Ray looked mortified at the thought; having a girlfriend had scared him, he'd never contemplated having a boyfriend.

Chapter Nineteen
The Nativity

Christmas break was just around the corner and so loomed the end of term. Everyone was in high spirits, dressed in cosy festive jumpers and Christmas hats. The parents clambered into the packed assembly hall, cordially greeting one another before taking their seats.

Veronica was overly pleased with herself as she had arrived early, gaining herself a front row seat for Ray's big debut – his one BIG line. She was so excited for him; it was the first time he had actually agreed to participate in the school Nativity. Her phone was fully charged set to capture this moment.

The local newspaper's journalist Parker, sat next to her quietly sieving he had been put on this project. He was never going to be late again he thought.

Smiling through years 1–4's inharmonious choirs symphonies, a triangle solo, a barrage of poems and a Christmas talent show, Veronica settled in for years 5–6's nativity play.

The school had made an unprecedented effort this year, the entire hall was filled with aesthetically pleasing twinkle lighting and decorative befitting scenery. It was impressive and did not go unnoticed by the parents.

Mary and Joseph entered the stage reluctantly holding hands, echoes of ummms and awwws ensued, cooing over the cuteness. Mary's mother waved tearfully in the crowd; Mary returning with a shy little wave. They walked through sand scattered on the stage replicating a very dry desert. Looking theatrically hopeless, Mary and Joseph spotted an inn; they wandered over knocking thrice on the door; the speakers boomed out through the hall with the sound effects.

Ray pacing backstage only needed to appear at the inn door, say his line and slip away. He read and re-read the line in his head.

"There is no room at the inn!"

"There is no inn at the room!"

"The room is not in!" he repeated before going blank and hearing the knock at the inn door. The audience was silent as he was ushered into view. Veronica beamed at Ray with his grey woollen beard and mucky robes they made at home the weekend before last. Everyone waited as the moments ticked by. Mr Vega the music teacher appeared with a crumpled script prompting Ray loudly whispering, "There is no room at the inn! There is no room at the inn!"

Veronica willed Ray to say something, but she wasn't quite ready for what he was about to blurt out. Hypnotically transfixed on the fire exit, his eyes adjusted to what he could see behind the dissolving walls. Ray pointed urgently to the fire exit yelling, "STRANGER DANGER! STRANGER DANGER! Man taking girl!" He got louder with every time he repeated it. Some parents were intrigued at the adaption of the nativity whilst others were unamused by the rendition.

Mario the caretaker and a heavy-set dad that stood by the exit took it a little more serious than everyone else; they collectively decided to have a look outside.

Outside, it was as Ray had just described; it was every parent's worst nightmare. A silver people carrier vehicle with a sliding door was urgently being closed, a faint muffled cry could be heard as the door slammed. A man with wayward greasy hair looked up; he spotted Mario and the dad looking at him suspiciously through the fence edging closer; he quickly scarpered into the driving seat before wheel screeching off down the road.

The two men sprang into action and sprinted towards the people carrier. Alerting a dog walker across the street, Mario yelled, "Call the police! He's got a child in there!" They ran as fast as their feet could carry them, but the car was accelerating down the narrow road alarmingly fast. Just when they thought they wouldn't catch him, a council bin truck turned the corner blocking the road ahead, allowing Mario time to catch up to the fleeing vehicle. He slid over the hood of the car to the driver's side.

The man flung open the door to make a quick exit; tumbling, he took a few steps before Mario had him pinned to the floor. A cry from the car infuriated Mario even further as he held the man with the grip of 1000 men; he pushed his face hard into the ground holding back what he really wanted to do. The men in the bin truck fell out over one another baffled by the scene they were witnessing. After Mario had blurted out what the man had done; he had additional help; one of the workers produced some cable ties from the truck; they bound him none too gently.

At the same time, the accompanying dad burst into the vehicle nearly ripping off the door; his heart sank as a little blonde girl no older than 11 years was curled up on the floor, a hoodie over her head with a loosened gag around her face; she had been haphazardly tied with duct tape in the rush. He ripped off the restraints with his bare hands, freeing the girl. Clearly shaken, she shook with fear and confusion. The man scooped up the child into his arms; he didn't know the girl but for a brief moment she felt like his daughter; he was moved to tears. He removed the gag from her face and moved her far away from the vehicle. He whispered softly to her, "You're safe, sweetheart. You're safe!" he made his way back to the school with the girl in his arms, her little arms wrapped tightly around his neck.

Mr Went and other staff members had rushed down the road in horror as the scene had unfolded; disbelief was an understatement as onlookers relived in the moments that followed.

In the midst of the happenings, Parker, who was only reporting on Christmas Community Spirit, instinctively slipped out the fire exit; he caught the whole event on his camera phone. He was witness first-hand to an apparent abduction and could only think of the red-hot article that he was going to write up; this was front page material. He would be the talk of the office, get the date with the receptionist that he had been after and finally be able to write more interesting journalism. The seasoned journalists had always boasted that it needed to be the right place, the right time, but he never seemed to be there, but this time, he was! He was going to make this his career-defining moment. Parker started getting all the details of the witnesses that he would do follow-up interviews with as the police arrived and took over the scene. He turned his attention to the boy that had alerted them to the abduction. Where was he?

Veronica heard the whispers of the events outside and raced to find Ray. A heavily pregnant Lolly had taken Ray into the sensory office where she shielded him from the onslaught of questions from teachers and parents. Once Veronica was in the room Lolly left to find out what was going on outside.

Parker darted through the school to find the boy that had predicted the abduction; he began talking to parents and found out that Ray Vision was a strange, withdrawn child. Short Skirt Sally who had refused to send her child to Ray's birthday party earlier that year because he was so odd, had made it known that Ray was her son's best friend; they played together every day, and she was particularly close to Ray's mum, Veronica. Parker lapped it up, noting down every word.

Mr Went took control, gradually dispersing the concerned crowds. Mrs Wiggle made a strong tea for Mario who sat in the school office still in shock. His adrenaline still rushing, he could not stop nervously talking about what had just occurred. People were listening adoringly to the man that had just strong armed an abductor and saved a little girl, who was now safely in the company of a police liaison officer.

Veronica and Lolly quietly contemplated the possible implications of the day. They agreed on only one thing that afternoon, that Ray was the reason a young girl was safe, but for his quick thinking and taking action, it could have been a whole different story for the newspapers tomorrow. They praised Ray for his bravery; he revealed in the positive attention he was getting. He was a hero.

When it was quiet, Veronica and Ray emerged from the sensory office to make their way out to the car. Lolly watched as Veronica walked with purpose. Her heart felt heavy as she watched her friend leave alone to face the world; just as she turned to go back into the office, Lolly felt a crippling twinge in her stomach; she lent on the doorframe as a big swoosh of water cascaded around her feet. The babies were on their way.

Veronica ignored everyone as they asked questions as they walked through the school. She hurried Ray through in a desperate attempt to get him home. She knew that today was not going to be easily overlooked.

Darkness had set early outside, the chill of evening was just setting, when Parker spotted the pair darting towards Veronica's SUV; he quickly intercepted them.

"Excuse me, madame! madame!" Parker called after her as she hurried Ray into the car. She turned to the reporter with demonic eyes and pursed lips.

"I just have a few questions for you about your son and what happened earlier today. Did he know the man that allegedly abducted the girl? Was the event pre-planned? Does your son have psychic abilities? Is he able to see into the future? How about the past? Was you aware that he was special?" Parker ploughed straight in with the questions. Veronica shot him a look as Ray peeped over the chair at the persistent man with a phone on record shoved in his mum's face. Ray was confused and troubled; he wasn't sure what was going on, but he gathered it was about what he said earlier about the girl outside.

"Are you serious? You absolute weasel. Get out the way!" She slammed the car door, as he shouted to Ray asking him what else he could see.

"Can you see the lottery numbers?"

Veronica almost ran over Parker as he scrambled in the kerbside trying to get a picture of Ray in back. They sped away down some side roads. They sat at the red lights for a moment. Veronica turned to Ray wonderingly.

"'Can' you see the lottery numbers?" she asked curiously.

Chapter Twenty
Hollow Words

Tim cuddled Louis and Louise, one safely tucked in one arm the other in another, whilst Veronica and Lolly looked doe-eyed at the new dad. The twins had made a surprise appearance four weeks earlier than expected, the stress of the abduction had induced the labour that same day, yet mother and babies were strong and could go home just 10 days after their premature birth. Tim had surprised the two women who doted on the new talc-smelling bundles of baby joy. A clumsy greasy mechanic, turned germaphobe, delicate, super, stay-at-home dad overnight. He had taken to parenthood like a duck to water.

Lolly closed the kitchen door quietly so not to startle the babies. Sitting down at the table cluttered with a chincy flowered tea set, she poured them a cup of tea into chipped China cups. Veronica slid an envelope across the table. Lolly read Veronica's face expression; it wasn't good news. Sitting silently, she ran her gaze down the letter.

Dearest Veronica, I am in England for another eight weeks. I would like to see my son before I go back to the States. I miss him with all my heart and have much making up to do. Don't deny me the opportunity to make amends. Please get in contact. A son needs his father and a father needs his son. Kev.

Contact Info Overleaf

"Shh…sugar." She corrected herself thinking of the delicate ears in the room next door.

"I know," Veronica said stirring her tea more vigorously than normal. They struggled with the conversation; it was awkward.

"The audacity! What you gonna do?" Lolly asked. Veronica shrugged cluelessly.

"That's why I'm here! I knew you'd tell me straight," Veronica replied. Lolly stared at the insincere cryptic letter.

"The so and so has seen the newspapers!"

"Wants to cash in!" she continued.

"Never been interested in Ray a day in his life. Simple as that, Vee!" Lolly paced the kitchen delivering one insult after the other as quietly as she could; she never held back her true feelings especially when it came to Kevin the 'Actor'; she had always had his cards, seen through the wholly bogus façade.

"Any day now that job offer is going to come through," she badly imitated Kevin's voice, as she carried on.

"I'm just off for a month to go and be an extra in Emmerdale – still waiting for that episode to air!" Which was highly suspicious she thought never bringing home a penny.

"Sheep tax – my elbow!"

Veronica being young and in love never questioned her bae, his intentions according to her was always for the good of their future. Little did Veronica expect that he would be out the door faster than an Olympic athlete sprinting to the finishing line, leaving her to raise their child alone.

"I thought the same." Veronica sighed.

She held her head in her hands; she always did what she had thought was best for Ray, but right at that moment, she had no clue what that would be. She knew what she wanted to do. Rip up the letter and pretend it never arrived.

They had all been overwhelmed with the national media coverage Ray had received for his valiant part in foiling a serial predator wanted in connection with seven abductions spanning two years, and the scepticism of how he knew the abduction was taking place. The events of the day changed depending on who you asked – some say it took 10 men to subdue the abductor, others say he gave up voluntarily. The one that particularly tickled Veronica was a parent who was sitting four chairs down from her, claimed they were the one who saw it happening first, but Ray had beat him to the post and let everyone know before he got a chance. The headlines varied as well.

'Boy Predicts Abduction in Battersea.'

'Mother Conspires with Abductor for Newspaper op.'

'Little Local Hero Foils Abduction.'

'Boy Witnesses Abduction and Calmly Goes on Stage to Deliver Lines.'

The very last thing that Ray needed now on top of the journalists and photographers cropping up outside the school just to get a minute of their time or snap a picture of the local hero, was a scrupulous father hungry for fame.

Veronica's consciousness elbowed her in the stomach. She felt sick. She didn't want to keep him from a dad that may have changed and that may be a positive influence in his life.

Veronica understood Kevin was a stranger to Ray; he was just an old picture that sat in a dusty book that rarely saw the light of day. But things could be so different she contemplated. Ray for the first time in his life could have two parents.

Veronica thought whilst Lolly talked at her; she took in very little of the background noise as she lived possible scenarios that may happen, should she allow Kevin back into their lives? She nodded in all the right places, enough for Lolly to think she was listening. The most astute of children would be confused she thought, an emotional gut-wrench experience for anyone at any age, even an adult would be struck by an absent father popping up out the blue. With someone as complex as Ray with his newfound way of living, the effect it could have on his impressionable mind was unthinkable.

Veronica sat for a long gazey moment; there was no happy ending to this, of that she was sure.

Making one of the hardest decisions she had in the last decade she decided for now, she was not going to tell Ray.

Veronica full of belly butterflies and body tingles, called the number on the letter; she was to meet with Kevin in a few days at a coffee shop in the high street to talk. Lolly whilst severely not in agreeance, supported her decision. She had handed her a card before she left with a nod of approval; Veronica knew what she wanted her to do.

Chapter Twenty-One
Indecent Exposure

Veronica delayed her arrival at the coffee shop; the last thing she wanted was to be waiting around for Kevin to rock up to the table. She hung around outside in the fine rain, staking out the coffee shop. Seeing a familiar face in a black waxed jacket, Kevin looked well, older but well. This annoyed her, how dare he look well after the years of abandonment, fully aware how that she hadn't aged well, she felt a sting of tears at the unfairness of it all. She took a deep breath; she was going to get this over and done with.

Kevin sat leaning back flirtishly on his chair ordering a cappuccino with 'extra froth' laughing cheekily at the plump, attractive waitress. Veronica shook her head; the guy was a fiend, hadn't changed one little bit. He stood to attention when Veronica approached the table. He smiled and held out a chair for her, which she graciously accepted. Kevin was grinning like a Cheshire cat; Veronica wasn't smiling back; she just looked at him waiting for him to speak.

"You look good, Vee." Kevin smiled; Veronica shook her head; she wasn't interested in the small talk. She hadn't seen him for over nine years, yet he couldn't think of a better conversation opener than her looking good, when she blatantly knew she looked tired, stressed and dampened from the rain. She abruptly ended the chitchat.

"What do you want, Kevin?" she got straight to the point. Kevin taken aback sat back in his chair.

"I want to see my son," Kevin said in an obvious tone, baring his palms. Veronica inhaled deeply. The waitress came back over.

"Can I get you anything?" she asked, keeping a side eye on the man watching her. Veronica rigorously shook her head, unfazed by the obvious attraction they weren't keeping hidden. Veronica set her keys and phone on the table; she settled for the awkward conversation. She had so many questions that were unhelpful that she felt she wanted to ask. She willed herself to say nothing as it would only open up old wounds that she had tried so desperately to heal.

Veronica entertained Kevin's story of why he left, the feeling trapped scenario that she had imagined he felt for years after he left. She empathised with him as he lay bare his feelings, missing out on Ray's first steps, first day of school, first holiday and so on and so forth; she stopped listening after the first ten minutes of the rambling teary-eyed soliloquy. Notably not a tear fell.

"Can you ever forgive me, Vee? I just want a chance to be part of Ray's life again, be the dad I always should have been," Kevin said looking sincere.

"Why now? I mean you're heading back to the States soon, that's not going to work, is it?" Veronica asked. Kevin shrugged.

"I guess I just grew up, and I know that there is nothing more important in the world than my son. A long-distance relationship with my son is better than no relationship at all right?" Kevin replied. Veronica thought for a long moment.

"So, I suppose it has nothing to do with the media interest in Ray right now?" she asked mockingly. Kevin held his hands up in defeat.

"I've obviously seen the papers, if anything that spurred me onto make the move to send the letter. I been here a few months doing some work and been putting it off, putting it off, putting it off, then one day, I saw his little face and didn't realise he had, you know, problems!" Kevin said still shocked that he had made a son that had problems. Veronica was irritated by every word that came out his mouth. The only problem Ray had was his shirt buttons.

"I could be there for him, for both of you especially at this exciting time in your lives," Kevin said as he reached for Veronica's hands; she pulled them away quickly. She looked down into her bag and pulled out an envelope. On the table, she set out papers and pictures.

"Kevin Lee Cartwright," she read off the paper in disbelief, chuckling at Cartwright. Kevin shuffled through the papers on the table; he laughed a nasty laugh, his soft convincing face changed to a cocky, stone-faced stare.

"Ohio Community Theatre actor disgraced for stealing church fund flees, additionally he has a 12-month suspended sentence in Illinois for what even is that…'subterfuge?' suspected of bigamy and owing unpaid child support for THREE children across two separate states in the United States." Veronica paused to let Kevin take it in.

"Curious. This guy looks like you, Kev! Take a look!" Veronica read loud enough for the floating waitress and patrons to hear, before showing him newspaper clippings and screenshots from Facebook and Twitter. Kevin squirmed uncomfortably, his face turning a shade of pink, his brow getting shiny with sweat as his black curl on his forehead unfurled. Veronica slid a copy of a self-published autobiography that she took out of her bag. 'The Life of an Actor – K.L. Cannon' of which there was no mention of Ray. She thumbed through the paperwork reaching the most poignant part of the revelation.

"See yourself as a bit of a writer, do you?" She laughed.

"Ah! See the best thing about you, Kev, is your predictability. Same e-mail address for the last 15 years, should really start thinking about a completely different password and not variations of your own stage name, K.L. Cannon2020." Veronica squinted at the angry face looking back at her. Pushing a piece of paper forward, she'd highlighted a list of e-mails that he had sent in the last few weeks to literary agents and publishers.

"What kind of name is that for a book, My EX, Ray and his special vision." Veronica nervously laughed at him, knowing how close he was to truth.

"I see you been a busy body as usual, Veronica." Kevin scorned angrily, his top lip twitching.

"Offering paid interviews for a son, you haven't seen for over nine years; you must have lost your mind, Kevin. You won't be coming anywhere near my son; he's not a pay cheque. He's not a story to sell. He's a complex child that doesn't need a conman father looking to exploit him." Veronica picked up her phone that was recording and pointed it square in his face.

"I can see right through you! Come near us ever again and this video gets sent to every baby mother and ex, everyone that you stole from, every law enforcement county in the US will know where you are, where your parents live, your e-mail, your phone number and your real name, 'Kevin Cunningham'." Veronica's threat was clear. Kevin stayed silent, shuffling away the papers thrown around the table.

"Keep them, I have copies," Veronica said full of poise and confidence.

Walking away, she left Kevin grimaced, regretting not asking if he still had her mum's engagement ring that he stole all those years ago; she reconciled that she would never get it back even if he hadn't sold it, which she was sure he would have.

Eternally grateful that she had made the call to Lolly's ex-military intelligence officer turned private investigator uncle before meeting Kevin. Today, she could have easily fell for his tall tales.

Chapter Twenty-Two
Up and Away

Wearing a crisp pressed suit, Ray wore the clothes, they didn't wear him as Hasnat had often jovially remarked. The navy-blue suit, with the personalised buttons really set off jacket, he looked every bit the handsome man he was. Veronica unnecessarily brushed down his shoulders as he struggled with the top button; he never quite got the hang of the button business. Turning him around, she did it up with ease as she admired him, smartly turned out in his attire.

Lolly's twins, Louis and Louise, had grown up, tall and slender they were identical in every way, mannerism and appearances. They helped in the kitchen, cutting sandwiches and laying the table preparing for the leaving party. The fresh cream cakes were in abundance, and the strawberry lemonade flowed through the fountain that had twice needed a refill.

The doorbell rang – it was Hasnat's mum and aunts; they streamed through the door with plates of food covered in foil; the authentic smells of Indian cooking tingled the senses. It smelt delicious.

Lolly furiously pumped up pearl balloons; she arranged them in a floating arch just above the front door, a stunning welcome she agreed to herself; it complemented the shrubbery outside, which had been perfectly preened; the lawn had been mowed in stripes and the summer sun had perked the red sunflowers up to their peak.

Everything was organised with absolute precision especially with Mrs Taste giving the orders. Mrs Taste had retired many years previously meddling only slightly in the business now again; she had fully entrusted it to Veronica, owner and manageress of the very successful family-run business, The Stop Button. When Mrs Taste moved to Switzerland with her son and his family, she became a live-in grandma, or Oma as her now five grandchildren would call her. Every summer, she would visit the UK and stay the entirety of the holiday with her second family, the Visions, of where she was always welcome, she was their readymade mum and nanna.

The doorbell rang again.

"It's Hasnat and his dad," Ray called out from the garden.

They'd brought more lemonade and ice. Everyone looked the part in their party clothes ready for a good evening – a last chance to say goodbye to the boys. The house was full to the brim with family, extended family and friends. It was alive with laughter and chatter as they celebrated a new chapter in their lives.

A projector played in the garden on a big screen as they hunkered down to take a stroll down memory lane. Some sat in more comfy garden chairs, while others sprawled over the manicured lawn's neatly set blankets. The chronological timeline had been carefully devised; it was of Ray and Hasnat's growing relationship over the years – holidays, day trips and birthdays conjured up blissful memories. There were tears of laughter as the boys took their first trip to the beach together getting stuck in a pool of crabs and crying, a photo op that Veronica was not going to miss. There were overwhelming moments of pride as the boys graduated earlier that year, a video of Ray practically running on the stage to collect his script before he dived off the stage in embarrassment. There were classic shots of Ray drawing street caricatures and pictures of his art that had been used on filmsets.

Ray had finally secured a one-year contract with a possibility of extension with a major cartoon/film production company creating a new animated series. Hasnat had been Ray's No 1 fan; he had posted all of his work which had been followed and admired on his website he'd created for him, 'Through Ray's Eyes' he had aptly named it. Hasnat on the other hand had graduated with a double degree in finance and IT; he landed himself a job with the same company as Ray, in a different department working as a junior accountant. That suited Ray just fine. Hasnat could handle the finances and Ray would deal with the decorating. Together, the boys were a formidable team.

When the film ended, Veronica stood up. Choked, she managed a few words to which a hush fell over the party.

"Thank you all for coming today. Everyone who has helped contribute and make this party special, you're amazing, and we couldn't be more grateful to have you here as our guests. Today, we say see you soon to these two amazing boys, Hasnat and Raymond. You two have persevered through life's challenges and truly have grown from boys to men. We could not be more proud of you both and all want to wish you the very best of luck on the new chapter that you both are about to embark on. Be happy. Be safe. And come home soon," she said as she teared up.

"Can we all raise a glass? To Hasnat and Ray."

"To Hasnat and Ray," echoed the crowd. The boys blushed as they sipped their champagne glasses full of strawberry lemonade.

During the party, Ravindra and Adam cornered Hasnat.

"Mum, Dad, everything all right?" he asked politely. They pulled him aside and gave him a three-way hug. Hasnat's skin had much improved over time, and whilst flare ups were never far away, he could now get away with only creaming once a day. Hasnat laughed and embraced them both at the same time. Adam unzipped his inside jacket pocket; he handed Hasnat a cheque and business class seats for their flight. Hasnat eyes widened as he saw how many zeros were on the cheque.

"Dad – I don't know what to say!" Hasnat said, half knowing he would get something, but this was far beyond anything he had hoped for.

"Well, thank you is a start, Son," Adam said laughingly.

"Thank you," he said as he hugged them both in for an unexpected three-way hug again.

"Now that's for you and Ray to live comfortably whilst you're out there, don't spend it silly; there won't be no more," Adam warned. Hasnat nodded in understanding.

Ravindra drew Hasnat close and whispered into his ear, "Call me if you need anything! Fresh pants. Food. Quick chat. Anything," she said, and she meant every word.

Veronica sat alone on the garden bench as the party was in full swing. She sat stoically staring thinking of baby Ray. She knew he was grown now, and she had to let him make his own decisions; she'd just always felt overprotective of him because of his conditions, and now, he was a man that hadn't just disappeared. It scared her, nonetheless. Ray's Tourette's syndrome had gradually subsided as he had grown; they still surfaced every so often, but for the most part, he'd learnt through rigorous therapy how to successfully control them. He still had autism; this was there to stay; this is what scared her the most, his vulnerability. She had taught him well and he was cautious, but Ray always needed a guide, a steer in the right direction. Hasnat was the only reason she hadn't freaked out the moment he announced he was off globetrotting. Hasnat loved Ray as much as she did. They were good for one another. Together, they were better than any comedy duo; they were inseparable and completely adorable; they made a terrific couple. A fine son-in-law he'd make her when the day would come.

Veronica felt someone's presence. Before she turned, Ray childishly threw his arms around her from behind. He nestled his head in her neck. They held each other for long moments.

"Thanks for never giving up, Mum," Ray said.

"Mum! You're American already." She laughed.

"No. Thank you – you never gave up and that made me strong." Ray processed this and squeezed tighter.

"Just thank you, that's all." Ray sighed.

The party drew to a close and the guests slowly dwindled off one by one.

Hasnat sat on the end of Ray's bed; they had a fantastic, emotionally heartfelt party; it was so nice to see all their family and friends in the same place. It was the last time they would be seeing them for some time. Hasnat put his arm around Ray. He had long known Ray's best kept secret, and a secret it managed to stay. Ray often watched Hasnat as his heart would beat faster in his chest at the exploits of what was happening behind closed doors. The unbelievable stories he told him and the proof he offered up about what was within touching distance. Hasnat soothed and calmed Ray he was the milk to his chilly they'd laugh.

"Having second thoughts?" Hasnat asked. Ray nodded. He wasn't, of this he was certain; the adventure of a lifetime was not to be regretted this late in the day. Ray clicked shut his door; he didn't want his mum or any of the stragglers to hear what he was about to say. He took out a golden box from under his bed.

"I found this box of all my old stuff the other day. Cringe baby pictures, a bit of softbaby hair; it's soft, go on, feel it." He thrust it at Hasnat who turned up his nose.

"Bit of a rank thing attached to this peg, I dunno."

"Ew." Hasnat heaved at the sight of the 22-year-old umbilical cord.

"And this." He took a neatly folded piece of paper that Ray had accidenty ripped; it was clearly worn with age. Hasnat pieced it together. Veronica had obviously forgotten she had stored it away in the box.

"There might be an explanation why she didn't tell you. Have you asked her?" Hasnat asked. Ray nodded a certain no.

"I don't need to ask her; it'll only upset her before we go, you know what she's like. Nup, nup, nup," Ray mimicked a mouth with his hand.

"What do you want to do?" Hasnat asked.

"I want to find him," Ray replied.

"And if you don't like what you find?" Hasnat enquired. Ray shrugged; he had no idea what the answer was; he just wanted to see his dad at least one more time.

"This looks pretty old; he might not even still live there." Hasnat said in reference to the letter's address.

"Meh! I have to try! You have to help me. I can't do this by myself," Ray said looking desperate.

"I'm in. I'm always in," Hasnat said reassuringly; he would always be in where Ray was concerned.

Their colourful luggage cluttered the upstairs hallway. Four 25 kg bags and two flight bags were packed and ready to go. Veronica had meticulously packed Ray's suitcase for every possible weather scenario; he had learnt over the years to let her just get on with it, wasn't worth the mothering earache. Veronica had gone so far as to hide some sweets in his bags for him to find when he reached California and unpacked his clothes. She was going to miss him.

Ray and Hasnat left on the Sunday morning full of anticipation and expectations, holding secrets and hands they flew off into the sunset looking for their next chapter of life together.